DNA Weaponry

Project Stealthblade 545446

I0633162

Errol Hewitt

chipmunkapublishing
the mental health publisher

Errol Hewitt

Published by
Chipmunkapublishing
PO Box 6872
Brentwood
Essex CM13 1ZT
United Kingdom

http://www.chipmunkapublishing.com

Edited by Aleks Lech

Chipmunkapublishing gratefully acknowledge the support of Arts Council England.

PREFACE

When we are born we think that we are starting anew and that the things in our past lives are forgotten, but sometimes when we suffer we do not know why. Psychic powers are real. They can haunt you. Everything alive suffers. I have come to that conclusion long ago. Our physical nature dies, but the spiritual part of us we hope will live on. When we learn that one day we must die it makes our time here all the more precious. Maybe our life spirit records our experiences and after we die it will stay with us and travel through the void in spirit form to be reborn in a new world where we hope that there will be no more pain.

There is injustice in the world. The force is our essence. Our mental life is illusion.

Our DNA is a name tag.

Dedicated to all voice hearers and sufferers of mental distress.

Artwork by Susie Hawkins

Errol Hewitt

CHAPTER 1

Only a few with the special ability of *clear seeing* would be able to see the chaotic impressions of the rain on the visually enhanced holographic screen, which made distorted impressions of twisted demons with black weapons, and celestial angels with fiery white swords, at war with each other as they battled for victory in the celestial realm.

Zyi fumbled through the contents of the drawer, searching for evidence. The glow from the visual system radiated his texture with the incandescence of grid lines upon his face; the pulse and burn a soft warm sensation of heat, in contrast with the motionless impressions of the rain.

The butterfly in stealth mode, with motion detector on outside the office, taking 3 seconds to turn to scan the full length of the hallway. A memory card of information lay on the surface next to the projected image of a face; the clarity of colour shown by the quality of the mathematical sequence used, the name Theo Grey in red italicized font below the image. Zyi's eyes fell to the worktop with the incandescent screen. The memory card came into view and he swiped it off the table. Accessing the information of finances on the mobile station there was a hidden information document. 'This I hope is what I am looking for,' he thought to himself with a vague self detachment. It was of no interest to him personally...the information. The only thing that he desired apart from real live models of his obscure fascination with creatures that are extinct was the addition of numbers to his account, so he could afford the beasts in the first place. The motion detector icon flashed into view on the mini comp. His fingers move in a circle on the illusions, he selected...'View'. A picture came alive on the projected image just above his hand. 'Damn, the security network. They must have got an energy reading from the power used in this room,' he thought to himself.

The butterfly changed into attack mode. Two small blast cannons unfold from the armoury and turn to aim. Zyi uses the mini comp to target the movement of the men, then he fires five stun charges at the unsuspecting inquisitors. Two were accurate, knocking into them, they stumble, the blast shutting down their bodily movement functions; they collapse onto the floor in shock.

Zyi scans the image of the face on the photo projection into his mini comp, thinking that the image might be someone relating to the money scandal he was being paid to investigate. Then he exited the room with the memory card.

Butterfly, RETRIEVE mode.

In chameleon stealth, he blends into the scenery and runs down the corridor as the butterfly follows.

Butterfly, select: Energyblast. Strength 10.

The sealed window comes closer into view as Zyi fires the energy blast from the butterfly's weapon, which disintegrates the window and destroys a segment of the corporation's building, revealing the city's neon luminescence. Zyi jumps out of the Mega corp building, the gravity boot's control system and power enhancers come into action as the butterfly lands and attaches itself to its homing point on his wrist. He zooms through the night among the hovering traffic of the metropolis.

Nearing the Atom bar he reduces speed and follows the descent of people and alien life forms that land on the sidewalk- with them it is less conspicuous. The Atom bar is usually monitored by the W.A.S.P.S. (Weapons Against Society's Political Secrets.) The underground movement of nihilists. Rejecting authority, they take the law into their own hands. They have the use of weapons on their remote operating wasps.

The flux of people enter the bar. A haze of coloured smoke drifts on the cool air from the night's wind. Zyi walks up onto the first level, peering through the clear transparent stairs at the lights on the way up the staircase. The lights made strange patterns. 'This place is like a maze... Where is my contact? The sign was a blue dolphin and a red sun,' Zyi thought.

Walking through the rows of people lining the hall he entered into a fairly large room. A young girl walked by with a smile as a small blue dolphin swam in the air in front of her. 'This can surely not be my contact,' Zyi thought. Then he noticed her walk up to a man with a glowing red sun in his eye socket.

The corner of the building looking vacant, he approached with caution, releasing the the butterfly in stealth mode to hover in range. The picture of the butterfly's view was shown in his left eye rather than on the mini comp. His illusions were on at his fingertips to control weapons. "Silverfire," Zyi stated as he came into the man's hearing range. He looked as though he was in the military, a gray stern look with serious concentration lines on his face; frowning. Then he replies, "Do you have the data and any information?" "Yes." Zyi flicked the memory card into view briefly. The man's eyes flicker greedily for a moment. Then Zyi traces the card along his mini comp feeder-line, downloading the image of Theo Grey into its memory. "Extra information, an image relating to the firm," Zyi pauses before handing the memory card over and says, "And the icon?"

The man with the fireball eye pulls out an icon card with 23000 credits valid on it. Zyi took the icon as the security guards from the corps building make their way into the hall, "Found 'im."

They fire a stun ray at the area, stunning six people including Zyi and his contact. Then the little girl unfolds a vast armament of cannons and mini lasers. She fired at them. Built for war and tactical assassination. Three guards fall and the remaining two create shields of deflection around themselves. The stun ray shuts down as one of the guards drops the ray dispenser. Zyi fires a round of stun bolts from his hand weapon and an energy blast - Strength 7 from the butterfly into the corner of the building, destroying most of the corner of the transparent structure. A wall of fire erupts from the fire eye of the military man and through the shields of the guards, knocking them onto the floor, with sear marks scorched on their clothing fabric. Then he slips into Clandestine, disappearing out of view.

Zyi blasts off through the opening he created into the heights of the city, butterfly in Retrieve mode. The young girl walks out of the edge of the destroyed segment of the building and down the facade of the structure, using force attraction to remain attached to the surface. She walks off into the crowd. The dolphin explodes back in the building, shattering the glass outwards in every direction.

The night's steel wind was chill. The moths were in stealth mode to see if they could film a crime or track likely individuals that lead themselves into breaking the law. The controllers were paid well for any convictions.

Two techno moths were following Zyi through the network of hover traffic. One came close enough to him to fire a tracking bug the size of a speck of dust. It attaches on the side of his gravity boot's control system, unnoticed. Zyi realized the Moths were in pursuit on the visual enhancer, illuminated just above his right hand; the alert symbol flashing in the corner. Using the illusions with his fingertips to control the built in mini computer, 3x seekers DESTROY mode released from the containment pack on Zyi's left wrist. The three tiny seekers zip out and hover in orbit around the attraction device, firing mini lasers. One Moth blasted into fragments, leaving a trail of smoke. The other displayed an energy pulse weapon which sprung into life with a few shots of energy fired at the Seekers. An energy pulse sunk into the shield of one seeker, withstanding the force of the impact of energy power- no damage. The other Seeker was hit, damaging the defensive shields; it retreated back into the wrist-pack. Chameleon / STEALTH. Seekers, RETURN. He turns off his gravity boots, activating them near the ground. Landing near a steel fountain spraying sparkly rainbow drops of water in the air; sparking like fireworks. Leaving the Moth stalker miles above in the traffic. Slipping into the back streets, Chameleon: NEGATIVE. The cloak of invisibility surrounding him folds into the power pack on his back. MAP: locate.. current position ATLANTIS Sector, route to residence in ISIS sector -46km. Gravity boots active, RETURN. The grav-boots always take the shortest cut to the destination.

The apartment was near the new hover bar, just overlooking the dome. He had been three days in the ISIS Sector, part of the giant Metropolis; built from cities which merged together forming the Capital of the United Worldwide Confederation. The job was done. It would be time to move to another Sector again.

The landscape shimmered as Zyi approached the doors at the entrance to his apartment. Silently they slip open, revealing smoke drifting on the candlelight within the shadows. The hushed tones of an old singer playing from the music data cube; he did not recognize it. Niara was sitting on the side by the window landscape, gazing at the horizon. Turning, as he enters. Her cropped straight hair, patterned by shades of blue. Zyi, stood transfixed as her eyes met his.

"You are in danger," her voice a soft tone of warning.

"Why?" he said in an inquisitive voice, hoping her answer would reveal her presence here, or her intentions.

"You are infected by a DNA weapon. It is a matter of time before it will affect you.'

"How do you know this?"

"You were being monitored."

"By whom?"

"I am researching the weapon."

"What does it do?"

"Well, it locks on to your DNA then it allows demons from other dimensions to haunt you, affecting your mind and your experiences, disrupting thought processes, causing unbearable torment and suffering."

"I'm I supposed to believe this?" he remarked in a tired angry voice with no faith in the information she was desperately trying to convince him with.

"I am from a planet far away, on the other side of the universe and you are one of the many humans throughout some of these galaxies in this part of space that has been affected." Her voice, the same tone, seeming to bear serious implications.

"Can you prove that I am infected?" - not really sure if it was the right thing to pursue the conversation.

"You have to come back to Dimo, my home planet before the weapon becomes active. There is no other choice."

"I decide my own fate! I'm not going anywhere," Zyi blurted out in incredulity.

"I was sent here to intervene, before it is too late."

"I know it's the 10th millenium and we have discovered life on other planets in this nearby region of space. You say that you can take me to a far away planet, to cure an illness caused by a weapon that I am not even affected by yet. I don't believe you."

This made Niara smile. Then Zyi notices a small fairy, rapidly beating its wings.

The door to the apartment burst open as a high powered weapon was unleashed upon it. A small horde of metallic wasps swoop into the room in attack mode. Weapons target Zyi and Niara.

A voice spoke through the com link on the lead wasp, 'We know who you are. Give us the information we need and you will live. Who was your contact at the bar?"

"What bar?"

"The Atom bar in the Zinc Sector, you were there earlier."

"The man with the fire eye?"

"Yes."

"He was my contact, I don't know his name."

"What did he want?"

"A memory card."

"What was on it?"

"Finances of the corporation."

"Anything else?"

"I didn't have time to check the hidden information."

"Liar!" A shot of energy erupted from one of the wasps' weapons knocking into the side of Zyi's waist, burning his skin, knocking him to the ground in pain.

The wasps descend towards Zyi, their stings loaded with acid, they make to land on him when the fairy near the ceiling of the room begins a short spell incantation that creates a shield around Zyi, protecting him from their stings. Then the fairy unsheathes a magic sword which emanates a green glow and, flying into the midst of the wasps, begins slicing them apart into fractured components. Lasers are fired at the fairy and three energy bolts are dissipated by her magical defense. Two of the fourteen aggressors escape the onslaught. Zyi stands, a little unsure of what just happened; feeling the pain in his waist, he sits down. "Let me heal you," said the fairy. A misty yellow glow forms on her hands and seeps into the wound, healing the skin; the pain disperses. Not quite believing what he had seen, Zyi moves around the room collecting his personal belongings and putting them in a bag. He then leaves the building. Niara follows, "Where are you going?"

"I'm going to another sector, don't follow me, it is dangerous."

"But the DNA weapon..."

"I will be okay.' Zyi tried to sound reassuring. Blasting off in to the flux of hover traffic, he leaves her behind. Thoughts race through his mind. 'How could they have traced me to the Isis sector? What is a DNA weapon? Who was she? She said she was from another planet. Maybe she is ill. But the fairy, it had magic.' This left Zyi wondering until he reached the upside-down waterfall in the Osiris sector. Landing by the mosaic pattern in the seating area there were people talking of their own affairs, with laughter rising from some. The lights cast soft shadows; the lines and colours on their faces were clear.

Ascending the steps to the park, named in wispy lights 'The Park of Angels', where the trees grow, there was a different light that was warm. A thin mist curled on the ground, moving in the shapes of angels. Stepping onto the grass he felt the softness beneath his feet. Walking into the deepest shadows of the undergrowth so no-one could see him he scanned his body with a manual detector and located the tracking bug on his gravity boot. Feeding the location information into his bio-comp, using illusions to select the minute disintegrate impulse charge, the bug the size of a speck of dust was targeted. A warm tingle at the tip of his finger. RELEASE: charge. Target disintegrated. 2am... it started to rain. A misty shower of haunting droplets impact upon the leaves of the trees, and on the people in the park. Zyi's eyes went slightly out of focus as a momentary cloud of darkness obscured his vision, stirring a deep fear inside him that had been dormant since childhood when he lost both of his parents in the garden of Zyprus. Then a blanket of fire unrolled from the sky just above the trees with thousands of dancing lesser demons descending upon the park; intermingling with the mist angels, cutting their heads off with swords of ether. A great demon steps through a portal, green electric flames cackling around his clenched fists, his great sharp teeth glinting in the night.
"I have been waiting long for this moment, the moment to torture and torment you until you die. There is no escape now," the demon lord said.
A blast of green energy erupts from his hand and Zyi is knocked to the ground in unbearable pain.
"You will die slowly; in agony you will beg for mercy; and there will be none," the great demon said and then laughed.

The pain was beginning to intensify in Zyi. A wave of magical energy slammed into the demon stopping the pain in Zyi momentarily. The demon turns to face Niara. He raises his hands and releases thousands of small hellfire balls, which impact in a shower of sparks, their wrath dispersing on her deflective magical shield. Then she lets forth a beam of streaming silver lightning that strikes the great demon, opening a wound in the matrix of its skin where vapour emerges where there should have been blood. Zyi, slowly starts to pick himsef up as if in a dream where unreal things happen. The lesser demons converge on him, stabbing him with their burning swords as if his death was a thing they were holding back on; rather then inflicting serious injury they seemed merely to be inflicting wounds that burned like acid; their twisted laughter a low squealing of pleasure. The fairy came to his aid, slicing the small demons into vaporous mist, easing some of the torment their blades of ether were inflicting on him. Niara dodged a wave of fire by rolling underneath it, springing up to blast another stream of lightning that went wide of the great demon, striking a tree with a splitting crack. The great demon sent another wave of fire in bursts, catching Niara off guard and momentarily stunning her with a painful surge of heat where the impact had been. Falling to her knees she mutters the words to a spell that create a sheet of brilliant yellow light enveloping the demon and closing the portal that had allowed it to enter into this dimension; sending the semi-ethereal demon lord and its minions back whence they had come.

Zyi lay on the misty ground, his body in painful discomfort from the little demons that had been intent on wounding him to make him suffer the will of their demon lord. Niara knelt beside him, her fairy sheaths the rune sword and they both use their powers to heal him as some of the people that had been nearby walk over to enquire about what had just happened, thinking that they had just witnessed some new technology that was being used for a film production. Niara helps Zyi up and they shamble over to the north exit of the park, leaving the startled people in there without an explanation of what they had just seen. Locating a quiet back street cafe they enter and choose a table near the dark shady corner. Zyi, having not recovered from the encounter with the demon, in a dream-like state occasionally mumbled something that was too low for Niara to define exactly. He closed his eyes as a mist of angels and demons battle for the fate of the celestial realms. Sliding a ceramic mug of steaming coffee towards Zyi, Niara drops a small tablet in it. Zyi takes no interest in the hot beverage that is before him on the wooden stained table. Instead his eyes flicker around the interior of the shop avoiding any eye contact with anyone. Speaking in an almost low whisper, Niara mentions to Zyi that her apartment is in the Mercury sector not far from here.

"You must drink this." She motions with her hand towards the mug.

"Where.. am I?" His voice the sound of someone that was being held captive.

"We are in the Osiris sector," came the reply, Niara feeling that the information was relevant no matter how little difference it made for him to know that. The virus had become active. She knew this would happen and she did try to warn him. Slowly, he sipped at the hot liquid and the light in his eyes return to their normal vigour as the cloud of confusion lifts from his mind. Silence, then Niara speaks; "Now do you believe me?"

"I don't know what to believe.. The demon.. You don't know this but ever since my parents were murdered, I have always had this nightmare where a great demon would descend from a wall of fire reaching out with its great clawed hand to clasp around my neck, then...' Zyi thinks back and doesn't continue with his trail of thought. "...And then I would wake up in a cold sweat fearing for my life, not able to get back to sleep for hours afterwards. I was never able to remember how my parents were killed, but I have been haunted ever since... by the demon of my nightmares."

"The demon is real, nightmares are real, the weapon is real," Niara spoke with a knowing, reassuring nod of her head. Zyi speaks slowly but calmly, "I can't believe what just happened. The demon is my nightmare, nightmares are not supposed to be painful or real, there are meant to be forgotten."

"You have to come back to Dimo with me, there you can receive the proper treatment so you can live without the torment of the weapon."

"What will happen if I stay?" Zyi enquired.

"Well, the weapon will start by making you forgetful by reducing your intelligence, leading to frustration and anger. There are so many symptoms that will start to appear, including sleeplessness and weakness, leading to an intense suffering with no apparent cause. You will start to see demons and they will haunt you while you are awake and when you are asleep you will be in his hell surrounded by fire that burns your skin and inflames your mind. It is torture that no mere mortal can withstand for long. Words by a great poet from out of the galaxy who was one of the first infected once said about the condition, 'Only the sweet taste of death will be a release.' There is great harm in this DNA weapon, that is why I was sent here. You must accept my help."

Zyi looked at the hazy shimmer of light hanging from the ceiling illuminating the room, "I cannot go with you to Dimo, I have things to clear up here, maybe in a few months." He was not really sure whether to take this conversation seriously, after all she was proposing for him to travel to a distant part of the universe where he would be cured; it just seemed to be a little too far fetched for him to 100% trust her.

Have you forgotten what has just happened?" Niara seemed surprised and slightly shocked that he would dismiss her offer in such an off hand way. "You must realize that your life is in danger and you have no other option." Her offer seemed to turn from a suggestion to an order.

"I have a choice, don't I? It is my decision to stay, you don't have to help me." Zyi was tired and the sharpness of his words seemed to cut through Niara as if it were a knife he was wielding, not words.

"I will not try to persuade you. In time you will come to understand why the help I offer you is precious, because there is no way they can treat you here. In time you will need my help and I will return." Slipping a packet of pills into his hand, before she turns to leave, she says, "If the pain gets too much just take a tablet and it will subside. If you need to contact me my number is on the packet, but I will not be around for several weeks. I have some business to attend to. Avoid the park of Angels, the rain there is contaminated," With those words she departs from the cafe and heads in the direction of the Mercury sector; a sad, knowing equanimity pervading her atmosphere. Zyi puts the tablets in a pocket and finishes his coffee before nonchalantly leaving the building at a slow amble. Activating his power boots he ascends towards the hover traffic. Location.. Proton Sector. Power boots on full output he races through the traffic of busying inhabitants on their way to their own destinations.

The night was alive with the sounds of machines buzzing through the myriad of lights. Zyi knew the metropolis like his own reflection in the mirror. Living throughout the various sectors to remain inconspicuous so he would less likely be caught for some of his undercover operations, his hard work had led him into trouble with the justice agents, even though most of his work had been legitimate, though there had been deaths of innocent people. The explosion at the Atom bar had not been part of the plan, the man with the fire eye must have had to take necessary measures to protect his interests, whatever they may be. Was the information so important so as to cause such death and destruction?

The Proton Sector was nearing, the welcome sign a display of neon wisps that hung suspended in the night directing the traffic into various parts of the sector.

It was still night as tiredness crept up on him like fog drifting over barren plains. The apartment in this sector was situated high upon a towering semi concrete structure; the only way to get to the entrance was via gravity boots, no other mobile transport could access the area because of the entwining tunnels that were just the right size for Zyi to fly through. The area was difficult to locate because the tunnels were like a maze of pipes that didn't all lead to the same place. He had only been there twice before. This part of the sector was not on the mini-computer's database, so the map only showed some of the old sector's buildings. On his second visit he left marks that pointed him in the direction of his refuge.

Flowing like water through the tunnels the grav-boots eased him through the narrow spaces, the mini-comp tracking the direction. He stopped at some points to look for the signs he had left previously. The last curve brought him up into an open space where a crimson door shone in the darkness. He placed a hand by the deep red light of the door and traced a finger along a slender panel secreted in a pattern bordering the crimson glow. The pattern a soft green emanation overpowered by the rouge door at a distance so it didn't become apparent until he became four inches close, or when Zyi shielded the crimson glow with his hand. Slowly the thin polymer door slips open, activating the lights in the hallway. Walking into the main room, Zyi selects a meal on the food dispenser. Within the room lay boxes of things that he had brought for when he needed things for his safety at his new hideout. The beep sounded the signal that the food was ready. He heard this as he pulled out a small device which was a very expensive defense unit, state of the art. Picking up the tray with steaming vegetables, rice and beef he sits on the soft foam sleeping unit near the corner of the room to eat. Placing the defense mechanism on the floor, facing out and activating it so a silver shimmer shone for a few seconds creating a shield from one wall to the other, Zyi finished the meal and lay down to rest, vague memories of the day coming in flashes. That night he did not dream. The darkness surrounded him, there were no stars. Silence... then a far off sound... like a wave. Then fire. Surrounded by fire. It got hotter as the flames drew nearer. The pain. The burning of skin. Awake, shaking. The unbearable pain dispersed. He lay there as his breathing returned to normal. Unable to remember what was so disturbing about his nightmare, the imagery opaque, he gets up and turns the defense unit off and throws it onto the foam bed. Then he uncovers a box with silk cloth draped over it. Inside, another box. He pulls it out and sets it down on the floor. Opening it, he pulls out the display of twelve remote operating flies. Sliding the info-card along the feeder-line on his mini-comp the codes for the flies were made operational. Tapping the illusions with his fingertips he sends one fly to the Isis sector to monitor his old hideout, another to the Osiris sector to see if there is any evidence to suggest that what happened earlier at the park was real. The other flies he made active and sent them altogether out of the liquid window that could be opened by tracing a circle on it with the motion and pressure of a finger. The flies zip out in formation, waiting for the next command. Zyi takes the visual emitter from a bag and transfers the data of the flies visual perception to the main screen which springs to life, filling the space between floor and ceiling in front of him, curving off and fading at the corner of his vision on his left and right side.

The swarm of flies fly into the complex of tunnels and pipes. Looking at the map he had of his route here he retraces his passage and positions the flies at the various junctions leading to his new hideout; some of them he had patterns of flight determined so they would come back on themselves to patrol certain areas of importance. The various outlooks of the flies were segmented on the screen. One had reached the Isis sector. Taking over control, Zyi directs the fly manually to his old apartment. The door was closed so he steers the fly to a nearby niche to observe any activity: RECORD mode. Any motion in the area will be recorded. Fly Number:2 on its way to the Osiris sector, will be another 38 minutes. Zyi takes out the remote operating T-rex and positions it outside at the front entrance to the apartment, activating it to follow previous instructions; chameleon stealth and weapons loaded. Fly Number:2 soon reaches its destination. The park of Angels reveals no indication that there had been a great demon there, the only thing that seems out of place is the large tree that looks like it has been struck by lightning; no hidden or unexplained phenomena. Zyi closes his eyes slightly in tiredness and briefly sees something red flash in his view, he opens his eyes wider and turns the fly around to see... no, it couldn't be one of those little demons. But there is no sign of one. There were only a few people scattered throughout the misty realm, half asleep in their silent night rendezvous. Fly No.2 zooms in on a couple within hearing range to eavesdrop, hoping that they might reveal something of what he was sure happened earlier. Hidden in the mist of swirling angels the fly listens, not making a sound.

"There might be some evidence of what happened on the info-link by the afternoon. Maybe even a recording." The woman spoke with a hope that was not inauspicious. The man seemed reassured that his time had not been wasted by the sound of his reply, in which he said, "I heard about the incident three hours ago through a source that I cannot reveal... But, there are no signs of any. All that I am sure of is that there was magic used here, by whom or what I don't know. But the intelligence services from the justice department were swarming around here like flies earlier.' Moving his foot a step he crushes fly number 2, without realizing. The visual on the projection screen flickers into a background shimmer. A crackling sound assures Zyi that the auditory perception of the fly is also not functioning. Zyi, curses under his breath.

CHAPTER 2

The two in the park of Angels continue their conversation. 'You know that demons are real, you've seen specimens,' the man continued, lowering his voice at the end of the sentence to let her know that they should be careful with their secrets whenever they spoke of them. There had been some romance and the last time they were close, nothing came between them.

The woman spoke. "Demons are real. I know. They are walkers of the night and they live in your nightmares. They live on evil magic and cause pain and suffering to the soul. The containment field you trap them with is off-world technology. There are not many inhabited technologically advanced planets in our galaxy. The authorities might get suspicious that you've had dealings with other species unknown to them."

... A lesser demon continues on its intense mission to destroy the misty angels, it was infected ... Infected with evil.

"The only thing I need to worry about right now is that there are invisible forces at work here. Forces that come from other dimensions. Forces that can control your very existence and experience of life. I have sources of information." The man trailed off.
"I understand that there is an invisible force. But I don't understand different dimensions." The woman's voice was low in anticipation of furthering her understanding in an area she knew little about.
The man continued; "A different dimension is within us and outside of us, but the laws of our rational science are different there. In another dimension energy exists in another form... Where unrefined magic ether exists. That is where the demons come from. Time to time, seeping through the darkness into our dreams and making them nightmares."

...The lesser demon was counting the number of victories in a language known to demons. As he continued on his course of destruction, leaving a vaporous broken mist trail behind. His sword kept swinging and slicing at the ethereal shapes of the angelic realms, lost in some old forgotten battle.

"You say there was magic used here earlier? What makes you so certain that it was magic?" the woman enquired, with preconceptions of what magic could be. Preconceptions that allowed her to have a spiritual understanding and not a technological faith.

The man pointed towards the great oak. "Well, that tree for instance is split in two by something like lightning. Other parks in the Metropolis have lightning where it is controlled. This park is controlled by atmospheric regulation, otherwise it would be too dangerous to have natural rain because of the positive charges of the raindrops. The only thing natural is the mineral dust. There is never lightning in this park. Also, notice that other tree over there." He stood up and walked a short distance and motioned with his hand for her to see. "Notice the scorch mark with a deep burnt depression where a high concentration of fire at an intense speed bored through. There are other marks on some of the other trees, similar evidence. We don't use natural fire in this day and age, it's too unstable. This looks like condensed fire, now that has not been achieved in our scientific knowledge, but is thought possible."

The man scanned the area with an ether radiance monitor. "Dia, I still have no reading in this area. I saw it here earlier. It was an infected one, infected with evil so it had to cause death or pain if it judged anything living as opposed to their alignment, in other words it destroys anything lawful and will not stop to spare life. It was running around like a maniac slicing apart the mist angels. It is probably in the park on its intense mission to destroy the vaporous angelic beings that glide on clouds. Why would they not sense the deception of a mist angel as being a threat to them? It must be something to do with matter being different in this dimension; having different properties."

Dia saw a trail of mist going near through the centre of the park where it looked like the mist had been destroyed. "Over here," she said. "I think it went this way."

Noticing the trail, Kline sees the connection she was making and follows. "If it was infected it must have an alignment against angels, because demons do react to matter differently. When they see their reflection they become entranced. When they touch anything non-flammable, it doesn't catch fire and they experience pain. All living matter to them is pain in different degrees except fire, which is a pleasure to them. Even when they fly they are in mild pain. They are not supposed to exist in our world."

"But they do!" she replied. Then she pointed to the lesser demon hacking at heads randomly, keeping what seemed to be a count in its demonic language. There was a pattern in the mist which accounted for the display of a swinging sword and ruthless determinism.

"Ah, thought we might come across one." He blasted a bolt of water at the little demon and missed. The lesser demon turned around and threw a green hellfire into him, sending him reeling into the undergrowth, failing to dodge it, tripping over in the process. He gets up slowly, in shock and pain, surprised that the demon had magic. By this time the woman had grabbed the water gun and fired at the demon, missing with two shots as it flew off into the sector. The fear of water broke the enchantment it had with the mist angels.

Kline, wincing in pain because the hellfire had glanced his side, said, "Well, that is great, now it's loose in the metropolis."

"You shouldn't have missed," Dia stated, as if as a man he was not living up to what was expected of him.

"I've never come across one with magic before, it took me by surprise," Kline said, defending his integrity.

Kline took the bolt gun from Dia saying, "This one is more dangerous with magic. I might need your help."

"Well, let's try to not let this one get away then." Her boots hum into response.

They both zoom up over the trees and leave the park of Angels, going into the urban jungle in pursuit of the lesser demon. Chaos was sure to follow.

The little demon with ether sword in hand flew into the flux of hover traffic slicing at the people on their way to their destinations, making deep burning cuts which caused pain and brought cries of distress.

Kline noticed the disturbance in the hover traffic. He and Dia fly over. Kline fires three bolts of water, one accurate, sending the demon flying back but not freezing it. A wall of ether fire soars from the demon's hand and narrowly misses Kline and Dia, continuing a hundred yards before crackling into vapour. Then the little demon zipped out of the hover lane blasting a burst of ether fire behind him. The ether scorches the clothing fabric of some of the people watching what was going on as Kline dodges the edge of the fire curve and boosts speed in pursuit of the demon, firing bolts of water with three successive hits, knocking it off course and sending the little demon crashing into the ice sculpture of a centaur outside the shop of 'Long Forgotten Things.' The lesser demon flapped its wings and hovered by the window looking in. A circle of multi-coloured blue fire sparks and revolves in patterns, heat emanating from the energy. The little demon's eyes go wide with wonder, for a moment it stares as if in a trance as the words in the fire spelled out 'Real Fire.' Then a voice for the advertisement spoke saying, '*Fire burns,* but not our real fire at just 12 credits and a life time guarantee.'

Kline lands six metres behind, bolt gun aimed directly ahead, pacing forward. The lesser demon turns, its red skin looking blemished and withered, its teeth reflecting a sharp glint of light, resembling a smile in an evil way. The lesser demon spoke... "Fire burns." A wave of a twisted hand not holding the ether sword and a swirling series of ether fireballs spiral out and collide into Kline's left side, knocking him down to the ground into unconsciousness, his two shots with the bolt gun going wide. Ether flames begin to burn into his skin before Dia uses the bolt gun to extinguish the ether fire. The little demon darts off into the maze of traffic, weaving its way through with gasps from onlookers as they received gashes from the ether sword, bewildered by the speed and the oddness of such a creature.

"I don't believe in the devil, it is an old superstition," one man says to another.
Into the underworld Giz, the lesser demon ventures forth, tainted by evil; flying through a complex of tunnels and old ruins going deep down into the earth. "The lowest legal building has to be so far above the ground level," says one man in response to the other, completely changing the subject. An orange fire burns in a metallic bowl on the floor.

'*Only the poor, lost, homeless and forgotten dwell here'* is scrawled on the wall in ash.

Giz lands and walks slowly from the shadows towards the light illuminated by the fire, not noticing the mild pain on the soles of his feet because he was enchanted by the flickering flames. One man turned and noticed Giz approach; "Oh my god it's a demon... Talk of the devil. Ha, Ha." The man with the hooked nose sniggers and takes a gulp of brown liquid with unmeltable ice cubes from a refillable tech glass, seated in a morph chair.

Giz reaches out a withered hand to touch the fire. The men fall silent and watch the little demon's reaction. At first Giz has a weak smile, and then he puts his hand in further and the smile broadens. "I don't trust a demon that smiles," the man on the short stool comments. The lesser demon withdraws his hand and it is no longer withered. Then Giz steps into the bowl and sits there cross-legged surrounded by an orange fire, ether sword in hand, arms crossed. "Fire burns," the little demon says, staring out with a smile.

"Well it doesn't seem to burn you my friend," the man sitting on a piece of foam close to the fire replies.

"Aren't they supposed to be dangerous... Demons?" the man on the stool said to the man with the unmeltable ice cubes.

"It looks about as dangerous as an old lady watering flowers," the ice cube man exclaims with a smirk.

"Offer it a drink." the man sitting on the stool suggests.

Unmeltable ice cube man puts down his drink in the tech glass on a plastic box then reaches down to pick up an unused tech glass by the side of the stool next to the antique air chair that he was sitting in that moulds to your body shape and switches the glass on by a press of a button at its base; it fills up a measure. He placed it in front of Giz on the floor by the fire. Giz lifted the drink up into the air with magic and the drink evaporates in a wisp of mist. With a wave of his hand the glass shatters. The man sitting on the stool was taken aback by the magic. He surmised that the little demon might be more powerful then he first thought. The man sitting on the foam says, "Well that was a waste of technology."

"Do you know how much they cost little demon? I've got a good mind to wring your neck," the man with the hooked nose who had offered the drink remarked.

The little demon spoke, saying, "Offer it a drink," really sarcastically.

The man on the stool laughs saying, 'It's even got a sense of humour."

"I think it is trying to annoy me." Spoken just before a few sips as the ice cubes collided in the glass like mini icebergs in an ocean.

"Is it intelligent, do you think?" the man on the foam says.

"It can't be, it refused a drink," unmeltable ice cube man remarked.

"Is it intelligent?' the demon points its ether sword at the man with the crooked nose. Then pointing at the man on the green foam says, "Do you think?"

"I think it is trying to make fun." The man's voice rising slightly and picking a bit of foam off, he flicked it at the demon, it fell clumsily short. Giz blasts a thin stream of ether fire from his sword at the small piece of foam, making it smoke with a direct hit.

"Did you see that!" - spilling drink and losing an iceberg.

The man rises from the foam and backed away from the little demon. The man on the stool exclaims, "It is dangerous. Slowly make a move out of here," whispering the end of the sentence.

"I'll do no such thing! I'm not scared of demons! I've got a good mind to throw my drink on it!" said iceberg man.

"Fire burns, it is dangerous." Smiling now, a ball of fire appeared glowing just above the palm of his hand, spinning. The other man was rooted to the stool in terror, a rising fear overcoming him. The ice cube man received a burnt, smoking hole right through his chest as he flew off the morph chair, on fire, certainly dead. Giz looked at the man on the stool then at the smouldering man and said, "I've got a good mind to throw my drink on it!"

Then Giz flapped his wings, zooming off deeper into the underground complex, his skin smooth as a newborn.

Kline wakes up in care, reaching a hand to his face to feel the tender skin that had been burn but was now completely healed. His side was still a little aching, otherwise he was back to normal. Dia was sitting by his side on a hover seat. When she noticed his hand move she looked over and spoke, saying, "You are lucky you blacked out. Apparently burning is not a pleasant sensation. It doesn't happen very often in this day and age."

"It spoke," said Kline.

"What?"

"The demon, it spoke our language. It said, *fire burns*."

"Are you sure?"

"Yes. Demons that speak are rare, they can have their own language but it is demonic, hearing a demon speak is not a frequent occurrence. I noted a hint of sarcasm when it spoke."

"It had advanced magic, you weren't to know," Dia said, feeling sorry for having a go at him about missing his shot.

"I think it's got advanced sarcasm. The magic I can deal with. It has only been here for 4 hours," Kline turned on to his side.

Dia then remembered one of her travels in the galaxy during the adventurous years. "I've seen similar magic on another planet in our galaxy. This planet is mostly tropical rain forest where there are certain tribes that conjure demons from their place of existence. The tribes are rumoured to be thousands of years old, and they claim to be descendants of a space faring culture that had technology and natural ways of magic. They live in peace, using the demons to experience states of transcendental bliss. Their physiology is sightly different from humans. Their skin is translucent and has a sheen like a rainbow."

"The Uto tribes. I've heard of them. They were being hunted by a cruel animalistic warring race, that would not stop to spare life, especially if it was good on a plate."

"They are supposed to be immortal," Dia points out, as if what she may know about them were things that defy explanation. "The point I was going to make was that once in a while they would summon a demon that was too powerful for them to control. A demon that had magic. Demons that have magic are not paralysed by water, you should know this."

Rising from the soft bed, Kline slips into his clothes, then picks up a tech glass and selects carbonated water and it fills up. Taking a healthy mouthful and swallowing he felt invigorated, remarking, "I never studied demons with magic, they are so hard to find. My research has mainly been on the containment fields that trap them." Kline slipped his hand into the small pouch on his side and pulls out three metallic green acorns. "These take about ten seconds to work. They need to scan the area once they are thrown at a target before they can operate. That is why I didn't use them. That little demon was so quick."

"Then you will have to think of some way to corner it, so you can use the acorns." Dia picks up her electric key from the side table and the half eaten sandwich. "Would you like to eat some?"

 Kline glanced at the alien mushroom filled roll and said, "OK."

Dia passed over the remains of her meal saying, "The mushrooms look small but they are really filling. They get bigger inside the stomach, something to do with their molecular structure that makes them expand in the liquid." Turning, she glanced at the fibre door then looked towards him and reminded Kline in a low voice, "8pm, this evening at the hover bar, don't be late." Then she opens the fibre door and walks out, leaving a trail of perfume behind her in the air.

CHAPTER 3

Someone in another dimension, a spiky horned one says, "He is really getting on my little toe. That demon is annoying."
"It's the same one that was reported to be dwelling in dimension 'Y122', apparently his name is Giz," said another female, a young smooth horned demonette with eye lashes in dimension 'X655'
"Why do you like him so much?" asked the spiky horned one.
"Because he is exciting. He was always getting into trouble with the greater demon in dimension 'Y122' - Nimordi. And he is tainted with evil."
"Tainted by evil?" the spiky horned one said, almost in a whisper.
"Yes, he has tasted the ether fire blood of a greater demon which makes him naturally more evil. And, he has touched crimson water, so he also has magic. I have been watching the impressions from this particular matrix gap which always watches him."
"Well, I advise you to watch another matrix impression. I find Giz a bit boring, he hasn't actually killed anyone since I've been watching and has been sitting in the fire doing nothing but staring at the humans." The spiky horned one flaps her wings and then flies off back to dimension 'X654' where the female spiky horned species live, not amused by her friend's liking of Giz.

Zyi had eventually fallen asleep in front of the screen and awoke in pain. His skin was burning, as he was being tortured by the flames of demons in his nightmare. 'It must have only been a couple of hours sleep,' he thought to himself. His skin looked normal and he couldn't understand why it was still burning now that he was awake.
Going into the bathroom where an old fashioned bath was and room for a particle sprayer, he undressed and stood on the rotation disc which started to automatically turn, releasing the particle spray wash, which covered his body with a warm hiss, cleaning him and taking away some of the memories of his disturbed sleep.
Drying within a few moments, the particles evaporated leaving a fragrant scent upon him. Still feeling tired, but slightly refreshed, because it was not quality sleep that he had, he operated the food dispenser to make breakfast. Within a few minutes a bowl of fried banana and coconut milk appeared with a beep to alert the hungry individual.

Sitting down on a foam cushion Zyi turned his attention to the main screen to check the current news on the info-link to see if there was anything about what happened at the park of Angels. The news reporter confirmed his encounter with the great demon and its minions. "In the small hours of last night a phenomenon took place at the park of Angels. Reports say that there was an appearance of a Greater Demon and hundreds of lesser demons. What exactly took place we are unsure about, but sources say that there was a battle involving someone skilled in the arts of magic who had banished the demons. How the great demon appeared is still not known. We have experts who say the only way it could have got into our dimension is through a portal. How magical portals work we are still trying to understand. We have a brief recording by a Moth controller that was at the scene..."

A picture from the moth's recording device showed the great demon sending forth bursts of fire. Then the demons were gone. Zyi closed his eyes and the demons were there, inside... whispering... He opened his eyes, the voices faded. The screen flickered Fly No1 on screen, picking up the motion at the doorway to his old apartment in the Isis Sector. Two officials with light blue uniforms and numbers on their badges, stun guns secured in tidy semi-strengthened plastic holsters at their sides, knocked on the door and rang the buzzer. Eventually they use the techno skeleton key with an electronic pulse, waves of electricity emitted, the lock invisibly opens. They walk in, the fly follows them and picks up their conversation.

"Apart from the blast holes and the fractured components lying on the floor there is no sign of him," the female justice agent said.

"Is there anything to help us track him?" the other agent said. "It looks like there was magic used here." The man pointed to the scorch marks on one wall.

"Or it could be real fire, by the looks of it," she observed. There was a faint rainbow effect on the sear marks and the male noted it down with 88% positive that it was magic, and magic is illegal on earth.

Picking up bits of the fragments of the wasps the female officer says, "They look like they exploded from the inside or something. This one looks like it has a bandage on one arm." With closer inspection the words, 'No pain, I'm a machine,' could be seen etched on its thorax; the abdomen was completely severed, one wing remained. "Seems like there could have been some trouble here."

"I agree," the man says.

The hushed tones of an old singer came from the music data cube. "Can you turn that off?" she says, as the lyrics suddenly say... 'And now I'm gone...' "Sorry, it reminds me of my grandmother the day she died. It was playing on the radio when I heard the news." Then she pulls out the stun gun and sets it to damage mode, firing off two shots which completely destroyed the data cube and the music stopped.

"You've got to control your anger, Agent Hamstead. I can't let you lose it... do you understand? Especially if I have to rely on you. Do you hear me?"

She pulled her arms up so her hands covered her face. Tears falling, she rushed out.

'It's gonna be one of those days,' he thought to himself, before leaving to follow her.

Zyi, a little bit disappointed, because he was going to go back for the music cube, lands the fly on the back of the cap the female officer was wearing, letting it be a tracking device in case they got to close to him, so he would know. -RECORD mode. Suddenly a wave of dread overcomes him as he rises to leave the apartment to get the next mission from his work source. A small demon flickers into view, stroking an ether sword against the reddish skin on its hand. Zyi felt his hand burning and cried out in pain. Then a deep voice surrounded with laughter echoes... "Soon it will be time to die." This freaks Zyi out a bit, then the pain and the demon disappear.

Zyi put on his power pack and hover boots, then made his way to the door. A momentary lapse of intelligence; Zyi cannot remember how to open the door. 'There is no handle,' he thinks to himself. 'How does it open?' he wonders, searching his mind for a logical explanation as to why he can't remember, and was it a code word?

He states, "Open." But the door remained closed. Zyi begins to lose his temper. In frustration he selects the energy blast icon from the butterfly's weapons, stands back and then blasts the door into fragments, leaving a gaping hole and scattered debris. As he leaves the corridor and out the exit he notices a small button on the side of the wall with a symbol of an open door next to it. 'Obviously the activate button to open the door.' He curses himself for being so forgetful and puts it down to lack of sleep.

The maze of tunnels was a nightmare because he kept double backing on himself in twists and turns, feeling a loss of a sense of direction. An hour later he emerges out of the complex into a different part of the area. Butterfly: /stealth mode/... Something was not right. Things were becoming more difficult in life. His skin would burn and his concentration would shift and he was becoming too forgetful.

The contact for more work was an opportunity that was out of reach, there was another force in his life, evil. Then the shadow demons drifted at the corners of his eyes, they were chasing him, so he ran before blasting off again, with the demons in pursuit. He fires blasts of energy with the cannons of the butterfly's weapons system, the blasts destroying segments of the buildings surrounding the area. No people were injured. Some were scared; his chaos was fleeting. The demons kept chasing him; he took destruction with him with four moths following his trail and more material being demolished as he fired upon the demons of shadow that were there to torment him with whispering words of doom, affecting his experiences of pleasure. Life was becoming unbearable. His skin started to burn again so he tried to think of a way to escape the torture, but there was no way out that he could see. Then it stopped and the shadows disappeared, leaving a silence that reminded him of the stillness of another world where the deserts were untouched by the noise of an industrial civilization.

"Agent Hamstead?" enquired agent Mann.
"Yes."
"We have a report of someone that fits the description of the man you are after. Apparently he has completely lost it and has been causing a disturbance in the Proton sector. There are two of our Moths in pursuit and they have been tracking him. Details of his whereabouts are on your portable comp."
"I will follow it up, but I just have to eat something first, then agent Hock and I will get down there and sort it out, we have many questions to ask that particular individual.'
"Okay, but I wouldn't leave it too long or he might disappear again like the last time."
"Yes, he has proved to be a slippery character. But, I would not be at my best if I did not eat first, I need the energy."
"You can always have a convenience pill. They are full of nutrition

and energy and apparently you live longer, they are really good."

"No thank you. I prefer something I can get my teeth into, not a chemical tablet that makes life easier because you can't be bothered to eat a meal from the food dispenser."

"You know they are thinking of making it obligatory for all agents of law to take these convenience pills because they know that our time is valuable and every second counts. If they do, then we will also get a pay rise. I think it is a great idea."

"I think it's robot food and I am not a machine," she says with a slight edge of agitation. Then she leaves the room and agent Mann behind, making her way to the eating area for a hot meal.

Sitting down at a hover table with a plate of chips, peas and fish she starts to eat with the fork in her right hand. Agent Hock walked over and sat down beside her and remarked on her strange looking meal. 'What are you eating?' he says.

"It is an old dish which was quite popular in the 21st Century. It is fish, peas and chips. The chips are made out of potatoes and the peas are vegetables that were abundant in that time period."

"You do have some odd meals agent Hamstead. With over 30 million combinations to choose from you go for the most obscure things I have ever heard of."

"Well, you know I like my history and it is really quite tasty," she says as she jabs her fork into a chip.

"That eating implement looks a bit awkward," Agent Hock remarks.

"It is called a fork. It is quite easy once you get used to it. A lot easier than chopsticks."

"Chopsticks, never heard of them. I think I much prefer the illusion wand for eating. That fork thing looks a bit dated." He flicks the portable computer open in his hand and projects the image in front of them, showing a picture of Zyi in flight viewed through the Moth's visual system. "That is our man," he says.

Agent Hamstead finishes the last pea and leaves the fork on the plate, "Lets go and get him then.'

They both leave the Justice block and set their grav-boots to go to the Proton Sector.

Zyi races through the human and alien traffic with no demons chasing him. He thinks to himself that the demons are real and safety is his only concern, but he realizes that his contact is near at a hover bar. Chameleon/stealth and the moths lose sight of him. Speeding up the boots' power, he heads to the local hover bar.

Pulling out an off-world technology air-pressure shape changing drug he blasts a shot on his palm. It spread quickly, altering his features, making him look like a Velurian, slender, with light grey skin and serpent eyes. Butterfly, /homing point (wrist)./charging./. Chameleon /stealth/ disengage... Landing on the pictorial floor he walked up to the bar and spoke in almost a whisper. " A man was supposed to be here... His name... Ricter."

The man's facial features did not change. Then the man said, "What drink?"

"Blue Electric" Zyi stated.

The man behind the counter taps a number, then pulls up a drink from the Holo-/Realism dispenser passing him a goblet sending forth bluey-purple tongues of electricity. Zyi sips the drink and walks away. Standing under a lens by a seating area he gazes up and the magnification brightens the stars so you can see the swirling fire like an ocean of larva on its surface without burning your eyes. He finishes the drink and notices a small information chip, moving with the tilt of the glass, in the liquid. One last sip and the chip is within his mouth. The contact details within the metallic chip held the information he needed for his next job. He turned around and noticed that there was a little demon with the ether sword in its hand sitting on one of the seats, and it says, "Soon it will be time... Time to suffer.' It stroked the sword in its hand and Zyi felt a burning pain on his left hand and gasps in horror, in pain. Then he throws his empty goblet at it and the vision of the little demon disappears. 'I've got to get out of here,' he thinks to himself.

Leaving the bar he heads out, setting the hover boots to the Elysium Sector, to another bar. Sliding the chip into the wrist access point the information appears in his left eye. Reading the information on the way to the other sector the Velurian guise morphs back to his original anatomy and countenance. No Moths seemed to be following.

CHAPTER 4

The little male demon from dimension Y3222 had red wrinkly skin and was under the real fire light to regain its wellbeing.

Kline, had studied them for some time now and knew their needs. Within several moments the dry wrinkly skin became smooth and the young demon had more vigour.

A thin membrane of water molecules surrounded the lost demon far from home, keeping it there, trapped, but looked after.

The other two little demons that Kline had managed to secure for his research were the only ones he knew on the planet... except the one loose in the metropolis with wings, advanced magic, sarcasm, and a resistance to water.

The real fire was switched off and the lesser demon sighed and started to complain in its language, specific to his own species, but Kline did not understand a word.

All three of the demons he had in the establishment were slightly different from each other, but the one he knew best was Ratty from dimension Y676766. He had named him that because the little demon could not remember its name; he had a long tail and tufts of hair.

Ratty was apparently smuggled from another galaxy and was the most expensive demon he had ever bought. Most of the money came from his inheritance, of which he still had a lot left.

This was his research facility and business. He had a license and lesser demons were his fascination ever since he was a boy, and now his dream of working with them was reality.

Kline opened the language book, acquired for an extra price with the demon, a chance he could not miss because demons that speak are rare enough as it is. He had dealings with other species, in this galaxy and beyond, that knew things about demons.

So far, he had learned from Ratty, the little demon, that his particular species didn't all have tails as long as his and they were not as clever as him, because he was always the quickest at getting people depressed in their dreams.

"So," said Kline, continuing the conversation where he had left off, in a hurry to visit the park of Angels, "You can affect people's dreams when you are so far away in another dimension?"

"And when they are awake, sometimes," came the excited reply.

"Why?"

"We like causing suffering and pain to other forms of life, especially humans."

"Why?"

"It is fun."

"Would you like it if I blasted you with water?"

"No."

"But, what if it was fun to me?" Kline said.

"I would bite your leg off and toast it on some real fire," came the reply.

Kline put down the demon dictionary and thought about the threat from the lesser demon, a bit disappointed. He was trying to befriend this form of life, not make an enemy.

"I wouldn't want to hurt you," Kline responded.

Kline then switched on the real fire lamp to invigorate the young demon and to reassure it that he was really a friend and would not blast him with water.

Ratty was enjoying the fire and was on his back with his tail coiled like a spring, moving up and down in an exercise type fashion.

Kline knew that demons did not eat and was quite amused when he found one of his sandwiches, with a bite taken out of it, lying on the floor near the other lesser demons he had contained. 'It must have reached out through a gap in the water molecule barrier,' he thought to himself. 'I must make sure that the barrier is secure in future.'

The room was specially conditioned to keep the lesser demons in. And, the only exit from the room was the liquid window, apart from the door, which was secure at all times.

The image communication system came to life and a picture of his work colleague, Harper, with his arms folded appeared. "Kline, another sighting of the loose demon, in the Atlantis Sector."

"The Atlantis Sector, how could it have got there so quick?"

"I don't know, but the Justice Agents are involved now. You are required down at the Justice block to inform them of demon capture."

"Ok. I will be about 30 minutes." With that said the image disappeared and Kline picked up two water bolt guns and slipped an extra set of metallic yellow Acorns into his jacket.

Leaving the building he took the ground route, because his hover boots were running low on power. He knew the route and it was not far.

On the way to the Justice block he noticed several people gathered nearby. Upon coming close to them one of them an old man approached him and asked if he was interested in *Youth*. "No, thank you," was Kline's reply, "I don't take drugs."

Ignoring the others he continued towards his destination.

Eventually he arrived at the department of justice. Walking in he informed them of his position in demon research and someone led him to a room where three other agents were in conversation.

"I'm Kline," he introduced himself.

"The demon expert?"

"Yes."

"Well, we have a lot of questions. One, where did this demon come from?" one of the men asked.

"I think it had something to do with the incident at the Park of Angels. One must have stayed behind when the portal closed."

"Brief us on the way, as how to catch the thing." The agent puts down his water; all four of them leave the block and take an express justice mobile to the Atlantis sector.

"You should be able to stun it with this water bolt gun," Kline informed them. "Usually they stay stunned for a few minutes, but this particular demon is quite resistant to it so we might need to use these..." Kline offers three green Acorns to an agent and explains how to use them, keeping the yellow Acorns that work faster for himself. The agent points out to Kline that he can power up his boots in the mobile. A gadget on the side held a charging device which Kline used; in under a minute his boots were charged to the maximum.

"By the way, the lesser demon has magic," Kline said in warning.

"What?" said one agent, choking on his sugar tablet.

"I don't know to what level its power is, but just take into account that you might be dodging waves of fire."

"Are you serious?" the agent asked, hoping Kline was humouring him.

"Yes! I am serious."

"There is only one of them," an agent said. "And they are small, shouldn't be a problem."

"But this one has wings; it's exceptionally fast, and can talk." Kline tried to sound cautious, so the agents would not be caught off guard when in pursuit of it.

"It can talk?"

"Yes, it has learnt some of our language already."

"What can it say? Yes please. No thank you. How much is the

candy?" came the sarcastic remark from the slightly older of the three.

The three men sniggered at the joke but Kline was not amused.

"It is not that polite. It is more dangerous then you think, agents!"

"Oh, come on, it will be a walk in the park." The agent coughed as a message came through... "Demon last seen in Emotion Park, Atlantis Sector, three people wounded."

"I told you it would be a walk in the park," the agent said, continuing the line of humour.

"Didn't you hear, three people are wounded. It has an ether sword."

"A What?"

"It will slice you if you get too near to it."

"I'm not scared, as a matter of fact I'm looking forward to it. I have never seen a lesser demon." The justice agent seemed like he was going to say more but the one with the moustache announced, "We're here."

They left their transport and headed into the park.

The park of emotions had a light show that was constantly changing into different shadows. Giz was sitting on top of a large glowing green sun. There were several citizens on the ground unconscious with burn marks on them from when Giz had blasted them with fireballs, because they moved too slow.

"Looks like there are more wounded," the youngest agent said.

The four approach. The agent with the moustache walks up quite close to Giz and says, "Will you come down from there little demon? We will not hurt you."

"Offer it a drink," the little demon said pointing its ether sword at one of the unconscious bodies.

"They need to go into care. You have hurt them little demon and that was wrong, now you will have to come with us," the agent said sympathetically.

Kline was ready with the gun, and acorns, standing just by the agent speaking. The other two agents made their way behind Giz on the other side of the green sun, one with a water gun. Giz then turns his head at the agents making their way behind the sun and points at them with the ether sword, saying to the man with the moustache, "They need to go into care," referring to the two sneaking up on him.

Giz blasted two fireballs at them, one sinking into the agent with the water gun sending him into unconsciousness. The other agent just dodges the ball of fire and picks up the gun near his feet. He fired off a shot at Giz, but missed. "Oh, I won't miss again," he says as he pulls back his hand to throw the acorns, in range, enough to be accurate. A shimmering field surrounds Giz as the acorns activate near the ether radiance of a lesser demon. Giz slices a hole in it with his ether sword and jumps down off the great green illusion fireball, with his feet on fire, bringing the agent down on his back with a burning chest.

Kline fires a shot of water at the little demon, hitting the wrist, making him drop his ether sword which landed point down near the agent's hand. "Oh, I won't miss again," Giz states as he picked up the ether sword. Within fractions of a second the sabre had pierced the man's hand leaving him not bleeding, or at ease, but in agony.
Kline could not believe the little demon was unafraid of water. Most demons feel threatened by humans so they have an animosity toward them. They always feel pain when they touch water.
A wall of fire sailed in spirals as it collided with Kline, burning with searing heat and intensity. He is knocked down to the ground as the fire passes beyond, his acorns falling to the floor, a bolt of water going up into the air in a last response to danger, then darkness...

Kline heard the report of the incident the following morning on the info link when he awoke in bed under a healing scanner, Dia by his side. She said, "Maybe you shouldn't be chasing demons that can use magic, they are far too dangerous."
"I underestimated it, that's all. I won't be that slow again. Next time, I will be ready. This can't happen three times in a row."
"This is not a game!" Dia remarked. "That lesser demon has killed people. You cannot let it be the fate of others as well."
"I am not the justice department. It is their job. The only reason that I want to catch him is because he is rare and people will pay credits for information on new species on other worlds in our galaxy."
"So you don't really care that people are dying, because you are the expert who leaves it up to other people to deal with the problem." That said, she turned to leave the room, then hesitated and said, "I should have known that you wouldn't turn up at the hover bar. I was a fool to think that you might even be on time," disappointment evident in her tone. She left.

Kline felt a wave of sadness overcome him. He felt that he had let her down and despite her way with words, which could sometimes be quite hurtful, he still loved her. Thinking to himself that he would make it up to her next time, he arose out of the bed and dressed, planning to go back to the lab to check on Ratty and the captive lesser demons.

CHAPTER 5

Upon reaching the Elysium Sector Zyi is updated with the information in the chip. Another retrieve mission, more data needs to be recovered with maximum stealth and speed. The corporation this time is in the Hades Sector. Zyi decided to go and check out the area before doing the job. Setting his grav-boots to go in the right direction he made his way to the destination.

Along the route he started to notice the shadows move again in the corner of his eye. His skin began to burn and he started to wonder where he was supposed to be going. Then a little demon came into his vision, flying beside him, an ether sword in its hand. It took a swipe and Zyi felt an intense burning pain in his arm, then the lesser demon disappeared and there was no wound where it had sliced him, just a severe burning pain. Turning his grav-boots to manual he descended from the hover traffic to land in a small seating area in the Mercury Sector.

Wondering why he was going to the Hades Sector, he started to doubt his state of mind, thinking that if the little demon kept appearing and if his memory got any worse he would have to go and see a specialist.
Sitting down at a table for two he slid his card in the groove and a drink emerged from the confines of the machine, together with a plate of fried Yaki, a weird creature that is not found on this world.
Things seemed blurry as images of demons were floating around in front of him. There was a whispering voice in the background which murmured something in a demonic language, then the laughter of many demons echoed in the darkness of his mind.
Everything turned to shadow around him, then a light started to shine and distant choral voices of angels descended through the night of the mind. It almost seemed like an awakening as the environment slipped back into focus, the fried Yaki still warm on the plate in front of him. He found a silver strip clasped in his hand, which he had pulled unconsciously from his pocket, and drew it up to his vision for closer inspection. 'Oh, I remember... Niara.... The tablets!' Setting one free from the strip he popped it in his mouth and cut a bit of yaki from the plate to help it go down, then decided to card slide another drink to finish the job.

'There was no need for medicine these days, tablets were a thing of the past and the medical scanners would have picked me out in the crowd of other civilians if I had any ailment known to man. but I don't feel in control... I keep seeing demons,' Zyi thought to himself. A mercury feeling coursed through his body as the liquid metallic smoothness of the tablet brought a sense of relief from the fear of dying, as another demon with an ether sword ran towards him taking a swing, then a dove appeared in his mind and Zyi felt someone clap a hand on his shoulder. "Zyi Mercuriel?" stated Agent Hamstead. "Yes," he replied.

She fired a containment wrap around him, and said, "You are wanted for various offenses. You will have to be escorted to the Justice Quarantine... Those tablets, are they off world chemicals?"

Zyi did not reply, but he saw a flash of a lesser demon stroking an ether sword, then a hover justice mobile arrived and Zyi willingly went with them to understand what was going on. 'When will I see Niara again?' he pondered. Total unawareness of the consequences of his actions could have led him into this situation, but he knew full well that he had taken several risks with some of his escape attempts from certain jobs. Anyway, the demons had gone. Things started coming back to him, the future prospect of intense interrogation loomed as they approached the main HQ.

'I have never heard that song before, the one with the jazz singer on the music data cube.' All Zyi could think about was Niara, and when they met, there was something about her that made him feel at ease.

Soon they were inside the building. Agent Hamstead took the gravity boots and pack from him and didn't notice the butterfly in transparent cloak mode. She didn't know too much about him... about the built in mini computer.

Imprisoned in a sphere that read reactions and fed them into the filter of psychological outcomes for the expressions. "Yes, a reliable lie detector." Agent Hamstead assured him his fate was sealed.

"Well, where shall we start? You've been quite a busy chap, haven't you?" she asked with a quality in her voice, a quality that seemed like she was going to enjoy this interrogation process.

"You have a long list of offenses and you are not on our citizen list," she continued.

Zyi had paid credits to be erased from the list years ago so that the United Worldwide Confederation did not know of his existence, so it seemed quite odd that she knew his full name.

Agent Hamstead, after looking at the information screen, said, "The reading from the chemical analysis says you have unidentified chemicals in your bloodstream and brain. Where did you get the tablets?"

Zyi, now more conscious and alert than previously, replied, "A stranger gave them to me, she said that it would help with my condition."

Knowing that what he said was true she continued along the line of investigation. "So, what is your condition?"

"I was told that I have been infected with a virus."

"Our med scanners show that there is nothing wrong with you."

"Things have been a little strange lately. I keep seeing demons."

"Are you sure that it is not an effect of these illegal drugs you are taking?"

"I have only taken one tablet today and I feel much better now," he replied after taking a deep breath.

"The lie detector confirms what you have just said, but you should know better than to take chemicals that some stranger offered you. Where did you meet this stranger? What is her name?"

"She was at my old apartment and she said that her name was Niara."

"And you have never seen her before?"

"Never."

"We will have to wait until the lab results come through on the tablets before I continue this line of discussion." Agent Hamstead paused as she read the text on the screen to re-familiarize herself with Zyi's long list of offenses.

"So, by this reading you have caused about 50,000,000 credits worth of damage to property with your operations. We have been monitoring you for the past two years and you have proved to be quite a slippery character."

Zyi smiled to himself in self satisfaction, it gave him pleasure to know that he had caused so much damage and her statement seemed almost like a compliment to him. "How do you know my name?" he enquired.

Noticing a slight smugness on his face she snapped back at him saying, "I am not here to answer your questions!"

Then another agent came next to her and said, "You are needed in block 4, your interrogation will have to wait."

Sighing, Agent Hamstead mentioned to Zyi that she hadn't finished with him and that she would be back.

"Don't expect me to be here when you return," Zyi said humourously.

"Going somewhere are we? I do not think so!" Agent Hamstead smiled to herself complacently.

"By the way, you caused over a 100 creds worth of damage to my data cube, so you have to repay me sometime, I will chase you up on it," Zyi remarked.

Being a little surprised that he knew that, she continued to walk off to block 4 without a word. Five minutes went by before Zyi used his built in mini comp and activated the butterfly's weaponry, blowing the central control system to pieces and setting free all the captives in the great room. Chaos followed as people tried to leave the justice quarantine, some under obvious medical conditions that could be contagious. Zyi recovered his gear and blew a hole in the building; blasting off into the city, the only thing that worried him was that he did not have the tablets and was fearing that he might start to lose his sanity. 'I must find Niara,' he thought to himself.

Giz found himself flying toward a great building with shimmering windows, the entrance a film of dry liquid used to stop the spread of harmful viruses in the air. He saw people passing through it and being inquisitive, followed three off world humanoids dressed in colourful garb through the doorway, which gave Giz a slight painful feeling as he passed through the dry liquid film. People looked at him a bit nervously, some not knowing what he really was and some not really taking any notice.

Inside, a great colourful sight greeted him as paintings adorned the walls of the art gallery, as people stood by admiring the skill of contemporary creations.

Giz hovered by one great piece of art depicting a scene of ancient Koolian - a planet in the milkyway. The artist himself stood by giving a talk and an in depth discussion on his latest work. "...And, it took me five years to complete," the artist reflected. "It is based on the civil wars of the world when their social and political system was in great turmoil, over twelve hundred years ago. They have had peace for the last six centuries and their political environment is much more stable now." The speaker, a man in his late forties, paused for breath.

"I've got a good mind to throw my drink on it," Giz stated.

"What did you just say?" the man replied.

"Fire burns..." Giz said as a green fireball appeared in his hand and began to glow. The man started to look a bit worried at the sight of magic and remarked, "Magic is illegal here on earth little creature! Do you want me to inform the justice agents?" With that said Giz threw the fireball below the painting and it started to burn up towards the fabric the great painting was on. "Oh no! Someone quick, put out the fire," the artist said, in fear of losing his prized work. "It's going to destroy it."

The green fire was slowly burning and some of the people standing by used their coats to put the flames out. Being admirers of the artist, they knew the value of the piece. Soon the fire was extinguished and Giz had moved on to other great works of art, putting some of the pictures to the flame, the ones he disliked receiving great intense burning holes right through them.

The gallery was in chaos and people were leaving the building in a hurry. The droids that worked there were busy combating the fire, and the agents of justice were summoned to deal with the problem.

Giz continued to set the works of art on fire until he came across one great picture that depicted 'Hell' by an artist called Morente. There, a great demon was surrounded by fire and lesser demons. Giz looked in admiration and felt a bit homesick.

Three justice agents entered the building and approached Giz with caution. One of the agents fired a containment wrap at the lesser demon, but Giz sliced through it with his ether sword and blasted a great fireball at him, sending him off his feet and flying into a wall. The other agents hesitated and called for back up, not daring to approach the lesser demon because it was more dangerous than it looked.

Meanwhile, Kline was back at the laboratory checking the captive demons there. "Hello, Ratty," Kline said in its demonic language. "Do you want a blast of some real fire?" he continued, switching on the machine and reinvigorating the lesser demons, making their skin smooth again, which gave them comfort. Ratty gave a sigh of relief and asked Kline if he could go outside for a while, but Kline said that he couldn't allow that, but he would take them to the rain forest dome sometime soon where in a few days they would be able to roam free for a few hours.

A message appeared on the main screen and Harper's image appeared and began to speak. "Hi Kline, it is me. Have you recovered?"

"Yes, I am a lot better now, thank you."

Then Harper said, "You are wanted down at the justice block again. Something to do with another sighting of that lesser demon. I advise you take a more advanced containment device if you are to catch this demon. It has proved to be more difficult than most to capture."

"I will take your advice. I was thinking of taking the spider net gun with its reinforced web."

"Good idea. Try not to miss." Harper's image disappeared from the screen and Kline took the gun from the wall hook. Making his way out he forgot to turn the real fire off as he proceeded to lock the door.

Soon, he arrived at the justice block. Making his way inside he approached one of the agents and said, "Kline here. I was sent for. Something to do with the demon that is loose and causing mayhem."

"Oh yes," the agent replied. Tapping a few buttons two agents appeared within moments and they took Kline to a hover car.

"This lesser demon is proving to be more difficult than expected, to capture," Kline remarked.

The agent with the scar then said, "Yes, we have been briefed that we should use maximum stun on our guns to disable it."

"I don't know if that will be good enough, so I brought a spider net gun with me."

"Well, I hope this time we can capture it. Apparently it has caused 100,000 credits worth of damage in the last half an hour."

The hover car came to a stand still and the three men exit the car and enter the art gallery. Inside, there is the smell of smoke and some of the paintings are scorched and ruined. The other agents in the building say that the lesser demon is on the top floor admiring Morente's work.

"Surprisingly enough he has not set fire to any of those pictures, unlike the ones down here."

"Maybe it has an appreciation for art," the agent with the scar says.

"I think that he is just lost in nostalgia," the other agent replied, guessing right.

"Well I think that we should get this lesser demon in a safe environment before it does any more damage," Kline said.

The six of them then make their way upstairs. Upon entering a large room where Morente's pictures were on display, Giz, the lesser demon, was flitting about from painting to painting, looking at the depictions of hell and the torturous images of work from the artist.

"There he is." One of the agents pointed out where Giz was hovering in front of a large canvas. Giz turned and noticed the men coming towards him. Kline this time made his way around the back where he could get a shot off with the spider net gun, hoping that the lesser demon's attention would be distracted by the agents.

Two agents fired simultaneously, with their guns on high stun, both shots hitting Giz. The lesser demon winced in pain, then conjured up several green fireballs and threw them at the men. Two agents went down burning and screaming as their clothes were on fire. Kline fired the spider net gun and a web wrapped itself around Giz. This surprised the lesser demon, but he soon cut his way out of it with the ether sword, before Kline could do anything. Then Giz turned on him and Kline felt a tinge of fear. The little demon fired a great fireball at Kline which he managed to avoid by firing the spider net gun at it, and the web made the fireball deviate from its course, stopping the full impact and sending a shower of fire nuggets cascading onto the stone ground. Then Kline fired another web, but the little demon quickly flew around it and sent three green fireballs at Kline. One fireball glanced his arm and set fire to the fabric, but did no damage to his skin. Then Giz flew off back into the main hall and out of the building. Kline thought to himself that at least he didn't end up in hospital this time.

A smooth, horned, young female demonette with eyelashes from another dimension was watching Giz in a matrix gap impression and admiring the male lesser demon's quickness and magic. She was infatuated with the charisma that Giz had and his daring when it came to fighting bigger opponents. A spiky horned one from dimension X654 came in to see her friend. "You still watching that annoying Giz?" she said as she sat down next to her friend.

"Yes, he has just blasted two humans and nearly a third. He is really exciting."

"Has he killed anyone yet?" the spiky horned one asked.

"Not for a while, but he is always slicing people with his ether sword. It is quite funny seeing the expressions of the humans when they get hurt," the smooth one replied.

"I much prefer a quick death, than torture," the spiky horned one said.

"Well thats the difference between my species and yours, we like torture on innocent beings and you prefer mass destruction as fast as possible."

"Yes, I suppose you are right," the spiky one said.

"Oh, look, he has just gashed another human. Did you see the look on his face?"

"I wish he would just decapitate them," the spiky one replied. They stayed together for a few hours longer and Giz flew around the city causing pain and discomfort to anyone he took a disliking to with his ether sword.

CHAPTER 6

Zyi, flew through the hover traffic and eventually landed in the Titanium sector where he found a discrete recreational area to gather his thoughts. A moth attaches itself to the underside of his pack and goes unseen.

Pondering what he should do he wonders where he can find Niara. The hallucinations had stopped now, but for how long? The tablets had worked and he was now beginning to feel a slight uneasiness in his internal self. Then from out of nowhere a small fairy flies up to him and says, "We have been looking for you. Follow me." With that, the fairy flies off and Zyi activates his power boots and follows.

Soon they reach a small building about 200 feet above ground level built into the side of a bigger structure. The fairy activates an open door security entrance code and they enter the building. Inside there was a nicely furnished room with plain decorations and furniture. Niara sat on a wooden chair next to a table. She smiles as he approached.

"You were right," he said. "I think something is happening to me that I do not fully understand."

"I knew in time you would see. But I had to let you experience the torment before you could trust me."

"I'm sorry, I was so harsh with you," Zyi says ruefully.

"It's OK. I should have known that sometimes things are difficult to acknowledge before experiencing the truth, but I had to try and intervene... There are other things that you do not know." She turned her head to look out of the window before pouring some water into a glass from a plastic jug and taking some tablets out of her pouch. Zyi then feels a burning sensation in his mind and sees a lesser demon stroking an ether sword on the couch, then it disappears. "I think I need those," he says.

She drops the tablets into the water and they dissolve, forming a metallic like surface on the water. He drinks it down and immediately the burning sensation in his mind goes.

"We must go to my home planet, Dimo. There you can be properly treated. Do you trust me now?" she enquired, knowing that she had earned his trust with her knowledge.

"Okay, it looks like I have no other choice. When do we leave?" he asked.

"Tonight. The spacecraft that will take us to Solarona is in this sector, but I have to prepare a few things before we leave."

"Good, that will give me time to clear up a few loose ends myself," Zyi says. There was something about her that made Zyi feel like he was close to her even though he hardly knew her... Something unspoken, or if he had known her in a previous life.

His mind was thinking of the DNA weapon. What was it all about? Why had he been targeted? These questions would have to wait. Niara picked up her small hand held communication device which contained her contact details and said, "Back at midnight."

"OK." He left for his apartment to pick up some things for his off world voyage.

Kline pursued Giz through the city and stayed just out of sight with several moths in pursuit to film the lesser demon in action. This time Kline was sure to keep his distance from the little demon, knowing that it could well cost him his life if he got too close. One of the agents had come with him while the others stayed, tending to the fallen.

The agent with the scar said, "How are we supposed to catch this lesser demon? We have tried everything within our jurisdiction."

"Can you get a license to use magic? I know someone who can cast," Kline asked.

"Maybe. I will contact the main jurisdiction office and request the order." The agent then tapped a few numbers on a pad and spoke into it; his superiors passed the use of magic for the next 24 hours to capture the little demon.

Contacting Dia on his communication device, Kline asked her to meet them. Within the hour Dia catches up with them in the Mercury sector. Within moments they see Giz gash another passerby with the ether sword. "It is time we caught this little nightmare," Dia remarked in anticipation of using magic legally.

Soon the lesser demon landed on top of a statue of a historical figure cast in rainbow stone from off world minerals. Kline blasts the spider net gun and a web wraps around the little demon, then Dia casts a spell which makes a shield around Giz so he can't escape. For a few moments they thought that they had him, until a swirling spiral of blue flames burst from within, melting the web and destroying the shield. Then Giz sends a wall of fire at them, catching the agent with the scar and Kline off guard and knocking them back and onto the ground. The agent was unconscious. Kline was lying there, mumbling something, on fire. Dia had cast a water barrier just in time to save herself. Then she cast a water spell on them both to extinguish the flames and Kline picked himself up, slightly shaken by the incident. He called for the medical team to tend to the agent. "You will have to try something more powerful to stop the lesser demon," he said to her.

"That was quite a powerful spell I used. Next time I will use a steel wall containment spell." She sees Giz fly off, "Quick, he is escaping."

They follow him for another 30 minutes, until he reaches the carnival. There, people were celebrating the dancing Goddess of Namor, an ancient tradition from another world where people dress up as monsters and mythical creatures to celebrate the birth of the Goddess. It was a relatively recent festival brought to Earth as part of the united planets union to integrate cultures all over the galaxy. "We've lost him for sure in this parade," Kline says. They look for him for the next two hours before they come to the conclusion that he had given them the slip and he could be anywhere.

Meanwhile, Giz had turned wrinkly and was in need of some real fire. Lost in the carnival he wandered, hovering just above ground level, flapping his wings quickly. There were many strange costumes and paraphernalia with the bulging mass of the crowd. Light displays made the scene alive with psychedelia and there were processions of monsters, with a glowing Goddess shining brilliant white. Giz took a disliking to the benign image of the Goddess and proceeded to fly up to her and sever her hand that held a candle, but his ether sword would not cut through the off world plastic from which it was made. Then Giz saw three little demons jumping up and down on a real fire display on one of the vehicles in the procession. Flying up to them and landing in the real fire his skin starts to become smooth again, then he speaks in his demonic language; "What are you lot doing here?"

"Oh, we're just sightseeing."

"I'm glad to see a familiar species," Giz says.

They sit in the fire and talk for about an hour, their languages being very similar. Then they go for a walk in the crowd, Giz flying just above the ground.

The carnival continues into the night and Giz suggests that they should go for a ride on one of the public transport hover trams. During their journey Giz blasts a few unsuspecting victims from the roof of the tram and the three little demons laugh with joy as one man's hair bursts into flames and he cries out loud. They continue this for a few hours before the tram stops.

The night was descending upon the great city as Zyi reached his apartment. The doorway was a gaping hole and inside the place had been looted; most of his belongings were gone. Zyi had forgotten about his memory lapse when he resorted to blowing the door off. Frowning at the damage, he turned to leave and noticed the info card for the operational flies on the floor. Picking it up he scans the information into his bio-comp and sets the flies to return in retrieve mode to Niara's apartment in the Titanium sector.
Thinking now that he had to prepare for his off world adventure, he checked that he had his credit card with him and set the hover boots to go to the Arcadia sector, where there was an all night surplus store where he could get some gadgets for his travels.

When the boots took him to his destination the shop was teeming with life and he looked around to see what he needed.
In a secure display cabinet there were various items that could be useful. Zyi thought that the two most important things were a laser knife and a fire kit, so he purchased them. Also, there was a night scope image enhancer, which had a range of up to a 1000 miles, which he purchased. Thinking the worst, he wanted to be prepared in case he was some how stranded on a world he was unfamiliar with. 'You never know,' he thought to himself. The last thing he bought was a container of convenience pills, 'Just in case.' All of these items he fitted into his belt pouch, then thought about getting some hot food at a hover bar before going back to the Titanium sector for midnight.

Finding a neat hover bar he sat at a table and slid his card in the groove. Selecting some Earth vegetables and off world meat fried in brandy, he ate heartily. The screen above him depicted the latest news, and Zyi caught a report on the lesser demon that was being pursued. "Some moth controllers have filmed him in action. Beware, if you see him avoid him. He is dangerous and apparently has the use of magic. This latest film footage shows him blasting fireballs at our justice agents. Two were seriously wounded earlier and are now in care. We have an expert on the case and we should have the problem resolved within a few hours. News out." Zyi stopped before finishing his drink as he saw the last image on the screen of Giz, stroking his ether sword, which brought back bad memories. Thinking that it was on screen and not his hallucination, he left for the Titanium sector.

Kline and Dia made their way back to the laboratory to check on the lesser demons and to have something to eat from the food dispenser. When arriving, Kline noticed something strange at the doorway. A thick black liquid was coming out from the gap at the door's base. Quickly he unlocked it with an electronic key. The door slid open and the place was a mess. There was liquid spilt on the floor, and things were strewn all about. The lesser demons were nowhere to be seen. He noticed that the real fire lamps were still on, and he cursed himself for his forgetfulness, suddenly realizing that the little demons must have gained extra strength from the fire which enabled them to escape.

The liquid window was totally destroyed by a real fire light placed to close to it. Kline looked out of the window and saw that it was quite a long way down. He thought to himself that the extra energy they had made them stronger, that was the only way they could survive such a high jump. "Well, that is just great isn't it?" Kline said, raising his voice.
"Well, you should have had a stronger water molecule barrier around them," replied Dia.
"That would have made no difference. I left the real fire lamps on for too long. Now we've got four lesser demons to catch. I could lose my license." Kline seemed a bit worried.
"Don't worry, they should be a lot easier to catch," Dia remarked.
"I suppose so. At least they haven't got magic."
Then the image of Harper appeared on the screen and he spoke. "I've been trying to get hold of you. Apparently there are more lesser demons loose in the city. Where they have come from I don't know, but you are required to assist the justice agents again. So you had better get down there."
Dia then suggests that they have something to eat first.
"It's OK, I will just have a convenience pill. You catch me up. I've got to get the situation under control." With that said he picked up

some acorns and headed out with a water bolt gun, leaving the Spider net gun on the side. Just before exiting the room Kline spoke to Dia, saying, "Be quick, I may need your magic." Then he rushed off.

Arriving at the Justice block Kline is introduced to two agents who inform him that they have been having some trouble at the carnival. Leaving to get there as fast as possible they weave through the traffic until they reach the area and approach the crowd on foot, looking out for lesser demons.

"Any advice you can offer us?" asks one agent.

Kline replies in a tone of warning, "Yes, if one of the lesser demons has wings, be extra careful, because it has advanced magic, which means you may have to dodge a fireball or two."

"Oh, that sounds dangerous. Will we be able to stun it with our stun guns?" the other agent asks.

"Maybe the other three, but not the one with wings. I am awaiting some assistance from a magic user who has legal jurisdiction to use spells, it will make our job a lot easier." Kline then trailed off as he searched the crowd for the little demons.

The carnival was in full swing and there were many men dressed in monster costumes and the women were looking like the Goddess. Music was being performed by off world musicians whose instruments were pleasant sounding and vibrant. Dia soon arrived, homing in on Kline's communication device. "No sign of them yet?" she enquired.

"No, but they must be here somewhere," Kline answered her.

One of the justice agents then said, "We've just had a message saying that the little demons have been spotted in the Titanium sector." Heading in the direction of the the alleged sighting of the lesser demons, they speed off in the justice vehicle.

The great statue of a condensed ice eagle loomed overhead as they entered the sector, traffic humming with motion. They soon head to where the little demons were last sighted, and soon there was a commotion by one of the weapon stores, on ground level, where suddenly a great blasting sound was heard as a great hole appeared in one of the walls, spraying debris. Ratty emerged with a great laser ball gun and turned towards them.

"Oh no!" said one of the agents as he was blasted into a smoking corpse. His colleague's expression turned to one of shock. Then the other three lesser demons come in to view as they leave the store.

Kline throws the yellow acorns at one of the little demons, the gadgets activate within 3 seconds and created a containment sphere around one lesser demon, trapping it. "Drop that weapon Ratty!" Kline ordered.

"No!" Ratty said, taking another aim at them. Dia mumbles a few words and waves her hand and a shield appears in front of them stopping the next laser ball. Giz then slices a hole in the containment sphere and the other little demon is set free. The three lesser demons decide to run to try and lose the trio that want to capture them. Giz flies after them. The other agent stays with his dead companion and calls for backup. Kline retrieves the acorns, then he and Dia pursue the little demons, being careful to avoid any laser balls from Ratty's new toy.

Chasing the lesser demons through this part of the city they soon end up near a space port where there are many ships for space travel lined up in rows. There were some workers here loading things onto a gigantic vessel, preparing to leave the planet. Giz and friends enter this cargo ship through the back ramp. Nobody sees them enter and Kline and Dia follow. Inside was a labyrinth of corridors and merchandise rooms. Kline and Dia were soon lost. "This could take all week," Kline uttered in frustration.

"This ship is huge," said Dia.

"Be on your guard! Ratty is dangerous with that weapon." Kline spoke cautiously. "Not to mention that other little demon with the wings."

Zyi reached Niara's apartment just before midnight where he notices his small swarm of flies, which he commands via the bio-comp into his pack.

Inside, Niara was sitting on a chair listening to a radio station. "Have you heard the news about the lesser demons that are loose in the Metropolis? They are causing quite a lot of trouble."

Zyi remembers the image on the screen at the hover bar, "Yes, it is a bit freaky. He looked just like my hallucination."

"Well, they are real, even your visions of them, though the hallucination physically hurt you they can't take your life by touching you, they can also send impressions of pain." Niara understood what she was going on about and Zyi now knew that there was more to her than what was revealed at surface level. She turned to the radio and turned it off, manually. "It is time to go," she said, paused, and then continued, saying, "Have you eaten yet?"

"Yes. I will get something to drink on the ship though, could do with some carbonated water." With that said he half smiles.

She picked up a small sack and said, "Let's go then."

Leaving the apartment they join the hover traffic in the designated hoverways. Reaching the space port they walk up the side ramp and enter into the cargo ship bound for Solarona, a planet in the milky way. A courteous worker showed them to their rooms and they left their belongings there, then headed for the recreation area to eat and talk. There were quite a few people around, but not as many as Zyi expected. Finding a comfortable sofa they sit down. Niara materializes a hot plate of sea food and rice and begins to eat with a hearty appetite. A great screen was on display showing off world sports where the teams playing against each other are armed with stun guns, set in an ancient building somewhere on Solarona.

The great ship soon comes to life and a slight lifting feeling could be felt as the vessel began to rise. It blasted off, heading out of the Earth's atmosphere and the solar system.

CHAPTER 7

The evening was fairly uneventful; Zyi and Niara only stayed for about an hour in the recreation area before returning to their quarters to get some sleep. That night Zyi had no nightmares and awoke the following morning well refreshed.

Going down to get breakfast he walked along the corridor towards the lift which would take him to the designated area, when a lesser demon appeared, flying with an ether sword in one hand. At first Zyi thought it was going to fly past him with no incident but it took a swipe with its sword, burning a small gash in his arm. He winced. 'I thought hallucinations were not able to inflict pain,' he thought to himself. Then three other little demons came running down the corridor and ran right past him. 'I think I need more medicine,' he thought.

Finding Niara eating her breakfast in the main common room, he sat next to her and said, "I think I need more of those tablets. I just saw another lesser demon and it cut me with its sword."
"The tablet you took last night should last for about 24 hours, so you should be all right until the evening. Anyway, there was an announcement earlier, there are four lesser demons on board this ship. I think that they are the ones that were loose in the metropolis, they must have somehow found there way in here. They should be taken care of soon, apparently there are two experts on their trail so the situation should be under control soon." Niara, took another mouthful of cereal.
"Thank God for that. I thought I was losing my sanity again." Zyi ran his finger over the cut the ether sword had made.
"We'll get that seen to," Niara said. "The medical centre is on this level. I passed it after taking a wrong turn on the way here."
When they had finished their morning breakfast they proceeded toward the medical centre. Zyi was half expecting to see a lesser demon come running at him with an ether sword, but there was no sign of them.
At the centre for the healing of afflictions Zyi's wound was seen to in less than fifteen minutes. The nurse ran a hand-held device over the cut and it felt like a warm glow as the wound sealed itself.
"Strange," the nurse said, "There is no blood."

"I was attacked be one of those lesser demons that are on board this ship, it used a small sword," Zyi informed the nurse.

Niara then added, "It is an ether sword. They are strange weapons and can burn right through almost anything."

"Well, I hope they catch the demons soon, this is the fifth casualty this morning." With that said the nurse tapped on the illusion screen to add some details. Zyi and Niara left and headed to the lower level on the ship where there was an artificial garden.

When they reached the garden which contained all manner of creatures, trees and flowers, Niara sat down on the lush grass. Above, a pulsing sun shone its man made energy on them. Zyi took a breath and sat down beside her.

"Tell me about your family" Niara said, running her fingers through her hair nonchalantly.

"There is nothing much to tell. All I can remember of them was that my mother had green eyes and my father had a black lotus hover car. The mysterious thing about their murder was that all power was cut off from the park of Zyprus where it happened; no-one saw a thing. I remember that two justice agents took me to a building and I was soon in the care of my step parents who still live, but I don't see them much. I don't feel that close to them. Then, there are the nightmares. I have the same nightmare, where a great demon descends from a wall of fire, slaying my parents and afterwards reaching out to clasp its clawed hand around my neck, when an angel of light with golden wings appears with a trident and a silver shield to protect me. I am always the same age, about four."

"That must have been really scary for you. Your parents are probably in a better place... You know..." Niara sounded sympathetic.

"I don't believe in life after death" Zyi replied quite coldly. A moth fluttered down to land behind them.

Niara, plucked a blade of grass and then said, "Where I come from it is common knowledge that there is life beyond this one. Once we reach Dimo things there might change your mind."

"I doubt it. I have no time for speculation or fanciful thinking." Zyi looked unconvinced that anything could change his way of thinking. "What about your life, tell me about it," he said to Niara.

She glanced briefly at one of the little flowers growing by her foot and took it. Holding it between her finger and thumb and spinning it around, she replied, "When I was young, about the age of three, I was taught the ways of magic. My first spell was an illusion. I could create light and by the time I reached six I could cast all manner of magical enchantments. My father nurtured my talent and I was soon to become a priestess. By the time I was twenty five I had achieved the blue flame ceremony, where I was accepted as a high priestess of divine magic, that is when I finished my training in magic and received the golden flame status... The highest level of priestess magic, which was almost unheard of for someone of my age, I was so young." Niara smiled.

"So, what led you to research the DNA weapon which brought you to Earth?" Zyi asked in interest.

"I was studying diseases. I have an interest in healing, and it is in my nature to cure malign illnesses, that is when I discovered there was research being undertaken on Dimo on the DNA weapon, and one thing led to another, now here I am."

"Agent Hamstead!" came the voice of an agent.

She placed her drink on the table. "Yes."

"We have a report from a moth controller who has a location on the man you're after. The number is on your computer link."

Spinning her illusion screen around she taps in her identification code and accesses her link. There, there was the number of a moth controller named 'Cortz'. An image came up; his face was young and he had bright blue eyes. The recorded image message played and he spoke; "Cortz here. I've been following the man wanted for crimes that I found on the criminal list. At the moment I am on a cargo ship called *The Mule*, heading for Solarona. He is here with a woman and at the moment they are talking in the artificial garden." Then there was an image as the moth flew around them and captured their faces. 'That's him,' thought agent Hamstead.

Making arrangements she and her partner go to the top floor of the Justice department to take a *space bird*, a high speed craft to catch the cargo ship, *The Mule*, before it reaches its destination.

Giz and his friends found themselves in front of a locked door which Ratty blasted a great hole in with his laser ball cannon. The four of them entered the cargo storage area and found boxes and crates, stacked in particular rows lining a great spacious room with several doors leading off from this storage area. They started to open some of the crates and boxes to find out what was inside, curiosity getting the better of them. There were several boxes with clothes and toys, destined for Solarona and some of the poor countries there. Ratty found a green curly, fireproof wig and placed it on his head. The other lesser demons were very amused.

Giz found a real fire mask which he placed on his face and it fixed itself there with flames of blue flickering an unearthly radiance.

The other lesser demons found a long silver fireproof cloak which one wore, and the other picked up an electric dragon that breathed fire, with a remote control, and some sparkly sunglasses.

When Kline and Dia were alerted to the breach in the cargo holds they made their way down there with caution, being on guard because they knew that the little demon with wings was extremely dangerous, and Ratty was becoming a threat with his laser ball cannon.

They found the door that led to the cargo area with a great hole in it. "Looks like Ratty's work," said Kline.

"I will deal with the winged one and you use the water gun and the acorns for the other three." Dia spoke with a slight fear in her voice. Walking in, they approached with caution. They could hear the sound of demon language behind some of the crates that were stacked high. Peering around, Kline saw that three of them were sitting down and Giz was hovering just above ground level, cross legged. They were a strange sight, as Kline noticed Ratty's wig, Giz's flame mask and the others, one with a long silver cloak, the other with sunglasses. They were talking in their own language as the remote control dragon took it in turns to blast the lesser demons, one at a time, with real fire.

"I think that they are having a little fun" remarked Kline when he turned around to Dia.

"We had better get the situation under control," she said in anxious tones.

"On the count of three," he said, "One.. Two.. Now!" They both turned the corner of the stack. Kline blasted three water bolts hitting the one with the long silver cloak and Ratty, stunning them, then he threw the acorns within range. Dia cast a sphere of iron three inches thick all around Giz, which totally surrounded him. The only one that was left was the little demon with the sparkly glasses, he made the dragon fly towards them breathing fire. Dia dodged the fire and Kline fired a bolt of water at it, sending the small metallic dragon into some of the boxes. Then, Kline fired a bolt of water at the remaining one, hitting it and stunning the lesser demon. By this time the acorns had activated and the two little demons were trapped.

Giz also seemed to be trapped, but then Dia noticed the little demon's ether sword had pierced the iron and was slowly cutting through it. "I don't think that the iron globe is going to hold him," stated Dia uncertainly.

"Try something else then," said Kline nervously. Dia thought of what else she could try to contain the lesser demon. She had little magic power left, and not enough to cast another sphere of iron. The ether sword was now half way to forming a complete circle that would allow Giz to escape.

Not being able to cast another high level spell, Dia made a wall of ice twelve inches thick around the iron containment wall, hoping that the ether sword would not be as effective. Kline produced another set of acorns and trapped the remaining, stunned demon. "I think we have the situation under satisfactory control now." He seemed pleased that it was not as much of a problem as he had anticipated.

Then Dia said, "Wait just a few moments, to make sure that the winged one is definitely trapped."

Several minutes pass before she was certain that he couldn't escape.

"I will go to the main control room and get us a craft out here to transport the lesser demons back to Earth," Kine said. "You wait here and keep an eye on them until I get back."

"Ok," said Dia.

Kline left her, certain that it wouldn't take long before the craft would be here to transport them back to their home world.

While he was gone, Dia heard a strange sound coming from the containment globe where Giz was. There was the faint sound of scratching and then the ice shattered outwards, showering the area. Dia could see the little demon's ether sword cutting through the iron. 'Oh no!' she thought, 'It is going to break free.' Fearing that once the lesser demon was free she would not be able to cast any spells because her magic power was so low after her previous castings, she hid behind some crates and watched uneasily.

Soon, the little demon had cut through the iron and jumped out of the hole he created. Blue flames flickered on his face making him look slightly more evil than he usually did. He then proceeded to cut through the acorn barrier containing the little demon with the sparkly sunglasses and it jumped about, free.

Ratty and the lesser demon with the long silver cloak were soon released, whereupon Ratty picked up the laser ball cannon.

The four of them then left the cargo hold and began to run around the ship again to cause disturbances. The remote operating dragon flew with them. The lesser demon with the sunglasses had the remote, and even though the dragon kept crashing into things he still managed to keep reasonable control. Dia then picked up the acorns on the floor and left the messy cargo hold to find Kline.

On his way back down Kline saw Dia coming up the passageway. "They've escaped!" she said.

"What! Oh, that is just great. How?" he asked.

"The lesser demon with wings used his ether sword to cut through the iron. I don't know any other spells that will contain him. We need help, they are too dangerous. Do you have any contacts with advanced containment technology?" she asked, handing him the acorns.

"I have a few numbers, but it will take them some time to get here. I think for now we should just keep an eye on the little demons and maybe somehow separate them to be able to trap my three ones, so the winged one can't help them, and maybe get that ether sword from him." Kline, took a breath, and then continued. "Lets go to the control room where we can view the screens and see if we can track them down and somehow get the situation back to normal." With that said they headed towards the front of the cargo ship to see where the lesser demons had got to now.

In the artificial garden Zyi and Niara continue talking. "I will show you some images of my home planet," Niara said. She pulled out a small stone from her pouch around her waist and held it in her hand. "I can store illusions in material objects, like this stone which has over a thousand pictures." Then she uses a command word and an image is projected from the stone. A lush landscape with a forest spreading out before the mountains was illuminated by a brilliant sun. "This is where I was born," Niara says. "The place is called Honeydew, because the trees in the forest have the scent of honey and on a mild day the whole area is filled with the fragrance." Niara tapped the image and it zoomed in closer to the forest where several buildings that were metallic could be seen, relecting the sun and sky. The image then goes inside the building where a young girl and middle aged man are casting illusions. "That is me," said Niara, "I was five at the time and my father was teaching me how to control some difficult illusions." Zyi watched as a small bird was flying about the room, dipping in and out of circles of fire, finally coming to rest on her father's hand. "Well done!" her father said. The bird vanished, leaving a wisp of smoke spiralling in the air.

"It's time for food," came a female voice. A woman then walked in with a tray of hot food and placed it on the table.

"That is my mother," Niara said, "She is a great cook and knows over a thousand different recipes, so we were always well fed." Niara laughed at this.

The four lesser demons came running in the direction of Zyi and Niara. "Oh, the lesser demons are here," said Niara, amused at the sight of one with a long silver cape, one with sparkly sunglasses with a small dragon flying over his head, one with green curly hair holding a laser ball cannon, and a blue flamed faced one with wings. "Its okay, they are not hallucinations," Niara reassured Zyi. Then the one with green curly hair blasted a laser ball at them, which narrowly missed. Niara created a protective shield about herself and Zyi as a fiery dragon's breath was unleashed in their direction, the shield negating the effect. The winged one waited there, hovering with an ether sword in one hand. Niara picked up the memory stone and Zyi released his butterfly, WEAPONS: active. Giz then let off a wave of purple fire which blasted right through the protective shield. Zyi and Niara dived to one side as the purple fire narrowly missed them. "It has advanced magic!" Niara stated in bewilderment. The remote operating dragon was upon them and breathed another breath of fire as Zyi rolled on the ground to avoid it. Ratty took another shot with the laserball cannon which went wide. Zyi then sent the dragon crashing onto the ground the with a strength 2 energy blast from the butterfly's weapon. Giz, hovered there and was just about to send a wave of fire in their direction when Niara cast a stun spell at him which stopped his magic and he froze, unable to do anything. Ratty fired another laser ball at the butterfly after watching it take the dragon out of action.

Kline by this time had made it to the garden and saw that Ratty was being dangerous with his oversized weapon, and threw the acorns in range which trapped him.

Dia had soon followed Kline onto the scene and saw Niara cast another spell to trap the remaining demons.

"I hope that your magic holds them," Dia states. "I've had trouble with the winged one. It has a high level spell ability."

"It's okay," said Niara, "The magic should hold them." Giz then shakes, and flies off at speed.

"See what I mean!" Dia remarks in an unsurprised way.

"At least we have the other three trouble makers." Kline walks over to where the three little demons are held with the acorns. "Hello, Ratty. Been having fun?" Ratty smirked at what Kline said and tried to blast his way out of the containment with the laser ball cannon, but with no success.

The butterfly attached itself to Zyi, and Dia says to Kline, "What are we going to do about the other lesser demon?"

"Maybe these people can help." Kline turns to Zyi and Niara, "We could use your help in catching the winged lesser demon, could you assist us?"

"Yes." said Niara. "Maybe Aylisha will assist us." She put her hand into her pouch and pulled out the small fairy and spoke to her, saying, "Find the lesser demon and send me a short range telepathic message when you have trapped it." Aylisha then went flying in the direction that Giz had gone.

A young, horned demonette with eyelashes, in another dimension, was watching Giz. Her spiky friend was with her and they were watching the little demons playing with the fire breathing dragon. "I wish they would cause a bit of destruction, they are so boring," the spiky one said.

"Give them a chance. There aren't any humans about at the moment," said the smooth demonette.

They waited for some time as the lesser demons were blasting each other with fire. Then Kline and Dia appeared and they trapped Giz and the other lesser demons. "Looks like they've been caught," the horned one said.

"It won't be for long," said the smooth one from dimension X655, "If I know him he will escape soon."

The two young demonettes watch as Kline leaves Dia to watch over the captives.

"He's taking his time, isn't he," the spiky horned one says. Then, the ice shatters and Giz flies out of the containment which held him and frees the other lesser demons.

"Told you," the smooth horned one says.

CHAPTER 8

"This is agent Hamstead. I am here on official business."

"Okay, you can dock in bay 3, the green light district on the east side of the ship," came the voice of the person in charge. The *Spacebird* landed with subtle grace. Agent Hamstead and her partner left the confines of her craft and they were greeted by employed personnel from the cargo ship's crew.

"Hello, agent. I am told that you are here on official business," one of the crew members said.

"Yes, that is right, we are here to arrest a man in connection with numerous crimes. His name is Zyi Mercurial; is he on your passenger list?"

The man pulled out a small screen from his pocket and examined it. "Yes, he is here in room 185."

"Could you show us to the room?" enquired the agent.

"Sure, follow me." he replied.

On the way to Zyi's room the three of them were walking along a corridor when Giz flew down towards them with a fiery blue face and he gashed agent Hamstead's leg with his ether sword. "Ow, what the hell was that?"

"I'm sorry, but we have a situation at the moment. There are some lesser demons on board and they have been causing minor problems. Shall we go to the medical centre to get that wound healed.?"

"No, it's not bleeding, it can wait." Then a small fairy zips around the corner and pursues the little demon along the length of the corridor. Agent Hamstead and her colleague look around and see them both disappear out of sight.

Meanwhile, in dimension X655, the young, smooth, horned demonette is watching Giz being pursued by the fairy when she feels as if she is being pulled upwards. Looking up there is a crescent darkness, pulsing with unholy light. "Oh no, a dimension slip," she thinks. Suddenly, fear takes hold of her and she tries to flee but the unholy, dark light pulls her up into it and she is transported out of dimension X655 into the mortal universe.

Giz turned and threw a small wave of fire at Aylisha the fairy, but the fairy was quick, creating a magical defense which stopped the fire. Aylisha then fires a light bolt at Giz's hand, making him drop the ether sword and a look of pain is hidden by the blue, flaming mask. Within seconds Giz creates a whirlwind of ether fire which circles, and then the energy is released at the fairy. Aylisha creates a stronger magical shield and is protected, but some of the energy damages the ship and alarm signals are sent to the control room. Giz picked up his ether sword as Aylisha drew her magic sword which emanated a green glow from the runes upon it. Red sparks fly as the swords meet and they are engaged in sword fighting for a while until Giz realises that Aylisha is highly skilled in swordplay and he can find no opening to wound her, so he decides to flee but the fairy throws a stationary spell on him and he halts. Soon, Kline, Niara and Dia arrive at the location and Niara casts a higher level stun spell on Giz and he remains frozen. "I think that should hold him for a few hours," states Niara with certainty.

Aylisha sheaths her sword and flies back into Niara's pouch. Kline picks up Giz and takes him to the cargo hold where the other lesser demons were. Noticing that the lesser demon still held the ether sword, he manages to prise it from his hand, finding it painful to hold, because it was dimension ether. He wraps it in a piece of cloth which immediately starts to smoulder and burn. 'Not a good idea,' he thought to himself. Finding a small oblong box made of onyx stone he placed it within and it seemed to stay relatively safe. Going back to the artificial park to retrieve the other little demons he controlled the acorns to lead them to where Giz was, and then went to the control room where there were crewmen. He informed them that if there was any movement coming from the cargo room and if any of the lesser demons escaped they must let him know promptly.

Returning to the common room Kline sits at the table with Zyi, Niara and Dia. There were two Ventilians and a male Trusian sitting by a nearby table. Zyi pondered what they could be doing on a ship that was destined for Solarona, where there was known hostility towards these two races. Dia and Niara talk of magic, both being interested in the natural form of the nature of spell casting. A concerned voice and image came on the information field above their heads. "We are sorry to inform you that there will be a delay to us landing on Solarona. There has been some damage to the ship which needs to be repaired as soon as possible and we will be setting down on the planet Zarkon, which has a breathable atmosphere. It will only be a temporary stay and all passengers are recommended to stay within the ship as this planet is mostly rain forest and could be dangerous to venture into. We will be stopping within the next three hours and the emergency repairs may take up to twelve hours. We apologize for any inconvenience and will try to make the necessary amendments as quickly as we can." The blonde lady with her hair tied back, in a yellow ochre uniform, zaps out of view.

Dia then says, "I know Zarkon. I have been there before. Remember, I mentioned the Uto tribes to you a few days ago." She taps Kline's arm.

"Oh, yeah. You mentioned something about them being able to achieve transcendental bliss using demons in some sort of ceremony" Kline remembered.

"Yes. I was there several years ago on an expedition. There were rumours of lost temples and undiscovered tribes. I witnessed first hand the Uto tribe's ceremonial proceedings, involving the incantation of spells which brought demons from their demonic realm to the planet, whereupon they were sacrificed and prepared into a powder that was blown onto the surfaces of the eyes, causing temporary blindness but giving them heightened experiences of bliss, which they called *minira*." Dia paused.

Zyi then stated, "I've never heard of them."

Kline spoke; "I know that they submerge them in water that is then frozen and they are left for a few days until their life force has gone. They then let the ice melt and extract the red dust which is the essence of the lesser demon."

"Thats right, " said Dia, "Apparently it is relatively painless for the little demons."

"It still sounds cruel," remarked Kline who had an understanding of the little demons who were his work and life. The four ordered some food and had something to eat and sipped their drinks until Kline said, "I had better go and check up on the lesser demons. Would you like to accompany me Niara? You might need to cast another spell to make sure that the demon with wings does not escape over the sleeping period."

"Ok," Niara replied.

Zyi was reading the latest news on the table screen and Dia had a small book entitled, 'Spiritualism and Magic.'

When the two reached the cargo area the lesser demons were still contained and Niara cast a reinforcing spell. "That should last for at least twenty hours," she said.

"I hope so. We don't want any unexpected trouble during the rest period. They could get up to all sorts of mischief," Kline said with a certain kind of admiration for the creatures. They both then returned to the social area.

The cargo ship held tonnes of supplies, with a capacity to transport three thousand passengers. As agent Hamstead found Zyi's room empty she selected Cortz's number on her hand held computer which was also a phone. "Hello. Cortz here." An image appeared of him on her device.

"I'm agent Hamstead, do you know where Zyi is at this present moment?" she asked.

"Yes. He is in social room 6, sitting by the sport holo screen." Cortz was then cut off as agent Hamstead and her partner made their way there after looking at the area map on the wall.

On arriving at social room 6 they found it lively with passengers having a few late beverages, and in one corner there was music confined to the space where people were dancing. Agent Hamstead programmed her hand held computer to do an image search of the room and a little light, about the size of a pinhead, shot forth from the device and zoomed around the room scanning everyone's faces. Around five minutes later the small ball of light returned with no conformation that Zyi was in the area. "He must have given us the slip," she said to her partner. Cortz then approached the agents and said, "Agent Hamstead?"

"Yes," she replied.

"I'm Cortz. The man you are looking for has just left with a female. My moth is following them." He showed her the mini screen of the moth's visual, and Zyi could be seen with Niara walking down a corridor. "Follow me. He is not that far away and could be going anywhere. We will be able to catch up with him in ten minutes." Agreeing with Cortz, they followed his lead and were soon navigating their way along passageways within the interior of 'The Mule'. Arriving at the entrance to the artificial park Cortz said, "They are in there. Sitting under the willow tree by the pool on the northeast side."

"Thank you for your cooperation, you will be paid for your work," the male agent said, and then motioned for Cortz to depart, so he walked off back down the way they had come, back to his room, while still monitoring what the moth could see and hear, to witness the proceedings with an avid interest.

The two agents made their way inside the park and saw the willow tree in the distance. They walked towards Zyi and Niara who were under a pale lit moon. There were others there enjoying the intimate setting, with a starry sky that was one seen from another solar system and which slowly turned from one angle to another, as the stars became viewed from different parts of the galaxy. Niara heard the footsteps approaching and turned to see the two agents standing over them. "You are under arrest Zyi Mercurial, for crimes against the UWC of Earth." The male agent zapped a field around him. Niara knew that it would be useless to explain the condition that Zyi was fighting against with the medicine and that they were going to Dimo, her home planet, to cure him. Within a moment Niara had cast a hypnotising spell on them and instructed them to release the field around him and informed them that Zyi had died in an accident on the ship and there was nothing left of his body, so they should return to Earth with the knowledge that he was dead. The agents turned and looked at one another in confusion for a moment, then Niara said, "Yes, it is a wonderful sky isn't it?" And the two agents agreed and walked off out of the park into the lighter part of the ship.

"Well, now we know that he is dead, we can make our way back to the *Spacebird* and head back home" Agent Hamstead commented. Her colleague affirmed the line of direction.

Meanwhile, Cortz had seen the spell that Niara had cast on the agents, as the blue energy passed from Niara's fingers to the eyes of the agents with a wave of her hand. Determined to get paid for a conviction, Cortz left his room to seek out the agents before they left for Earth.

The justice enforcers made their way to where the *Spacebird* was, a slim craft with the ability to travel through space at exceptional speeds. Boarding the vessel the agents contacted the control room to let them know of their departure, and the *Spacebird* blasted off into the blackness of space heading back to their home world. Cortz reached the docking bay where the ships were and could not see any Justice crafts so he tried to contact agent Hamstead by sending her a reply message through his mini computer, but her number was not available. Cursing, he contacted the Justice Department back on Earth to let them know of what had happened in the artificial park on board *The Mule*. When reaching someone he could talk to, all that they could say was that when the agents returned back to Earth, then they would undergo a series of examinations to reveal if magic had been used during the course of their work. Cortz was furious because this meant a delayed payment and more work. 'It looks like I will have to stay on his trail,' he thought to himself. Cortz, the moth controller, returned to his room to rest. The moth was in stealth mode with new anti-recognition hardware, which was more difficult to detect with modern technology. Landing the moth and orienting it behind one of Zyi's pouches on his utility belt, Cortz felt that it would go unnoticed and would be less likely to be brushed off. Flicking the old screen on that was about half the size of the wall on the other side of the room, Cortz drifted off to sleep with the moth's auditory record function activated, which he would scan through when he woke up.

Leaving the artificial park, Zyi and Niara walk into the temperature controlled decks of *The Mule*. "I think it is time you took another tablet or you will be up all night hallucinating demons." Niara reminded Zyi that now he was dependent on the medicine, which was for his own wellbeing. Pulling out the strip of tablets he pops another one out and swallows it. Ten more remained, enough to see him through till they reached Dimo. "I think it's time we got some sleep." Zyi said wearily.
"I agree. I am rather tired." Niara's voice sounded sleepy. They walk to where their rooms are and Zyi enters his sleeping quarters after bidding Niara goodnight, and she continued a little further down the corridor to her room.

The young smooth horned demonette with eyelashes from dimension X655 found herself in the centre of ring of tribes folk who were dancing around her, chanting some weird language that she did not understand. The great rain forest was pitch black except for the fires burning around the perimeter. A female lay on a wooden altar. She had been sacrificed for the demonette's imprisonment. The smooth demonette was suspended, trapped in a strange orange light that shone around her. She sensed that her captors were going to do something horrible to her if she could not escape, but knowing that she did not have any magic powers or great strength she was helpless to do anything in this situation. Time passed as the horned demonette waited, wondering what they would do to her, then she noticed a row of other lesser demons and demonettes encased within blocks of ice upon a ledge, and wondered if the fate that they had in store for her would be the same as these others. She tried to struggle free, but to no avail. After a long while the chanting stopped and a figure drew up close to her, he had bones tied around his waist and various markings on his translucent skin. He prodded her with a bone stick carved with a skull. Then he pressed it on her forehead and muttered some strange words and the bone skull became cold and the smooth horned demonette shrieked with pain at the touch of the cold stick. Within moments the demonette with eyelashes could not move any of her limbs and her skin felt cold. The chanting resumed and the elder shaman of the tribe took the young demonette from the orange light and walked to where there were great stone basins that had been hollowed out for the rituals that they performed. Lowering the horned demonette with eyelashes into the water, the shaman began his incantation as the other tribe members danced around with brands of fire in their hands. The demonette was then turned to ice, her expression of fear and pain frozen in a cold icy moment. Removing the block of ice with the demonette within, they placed it on a high ledge along with four of the other lesser demons and demonettes that had been summoned and imprisoned.

CHAPTER 9

Dia awoke to the bright sun, which she had programmed the night before to wake her. Getting dressed, she slipped on her soft footwear with an emblem of a golden eagle embroidered on the side. She would only buy clothes that were handmade, usually made by people from other worlds. She took pride in the fact that it was not machine made. Pressing the button on the entrance to Kline's room, she waited for a few moments until the door slid open, revealing complete darkness. "Kline. It is time to get up."
A grumpy reply followed, "Umm... I was just in the middle of a dream."

Dia strode over to the control panel and tapped a few buttons and the sun appeared in the room with a blinding dazzle. Kline rubbed his eyes and sat up in bed. He tapped a button a few times on the silver table by his bedside and a container of liquid fizzy apple appeared. He lifted it to his lips and took a few mouthfuls.
"We have landed on Zarkon and the repairs are being dealt with, so I thought that we could step outside for a walk after checking on the lesser demons. I have faith that Niara'a spell should have kept them secure over the resting period." Dia flicked aside a strand of hair which had fallen across her eye.
"I hope so. They are so awkward to capture, it would be a complete nightmare if they have escaped once again." Kline swept the covers aside and proceeded to get dressed. Dia averted her eyes and strolled over to the screen opposite the bed and scanned the information there.
"Oh no. It says that all passengers must remain on board for the next four hours before take off because we are not covered by their insurance policy." Dia frowned.
"It is probably a good thing. There might be some nasty diseases lurking within the rain forest, even though I would like to witness the ceremonies of the Uto tribes and maybe get a few more specimens for my work." Kline took another half-awake swig of his drink and wiped his chin as a rivulet of fizzy apple dripped off. "Lets go and check on our captives. The little demons should still be there." Kline downed the rest of his drink and headed towards the door fully dressed. Dia followed.
"We will get some breakfast afterwards, I'm famished." Kline's

stomach rumbled.

They headed down various corridors before reaching the cargo area. Stepping inside they notice that something seemed not quite right. There was a cool stream of air coming from somewhere. Looking behind the crates where the little demons were secured Kline lets out a curse when he notices that the the onyx box, which contained the ether sword that he should have taken with him was empty and that the demons had escaped once again, and a gaping hole was still smouldering on the far wall of the ship, which led out in to the dense forest of Zarkon. "They can't have got far, the damage has only been done recently. I'm going after them. They are worth several thousand credits, it's my life's work." Kline knew that Dia would object.

"Are you mad? It is dangerous out there, plus this ship is taking off in a short while, you don't want to be stranded here!" Dia knew from past experience that once Kline had made up his mind there was no stopping him.

"I'll be back before the ship leaves. Anyway, they have to repair that hole." Kline laughed, "I bet it was Ratty with that laser ball gun set on high power, they're clever little creatures really."

"This is no time to joke. You are putting your life at risk going after them and I'm coming with you." With that the two leave the ship through the breach and head into the vast sea of forest.

Zyi and Niara were having breakfast in the social room when the announcement came that further repairs had to be seen to and that there was a longer delay. "Typical," said Niara. "You just can't trust technology."

"It does have its advantages. I probably wouldn't be alive if it wasn't for some of the inventions that were made. I owe my life to some of these gadgets." He controlled his butterfly with the illusions at his finger tips and directed it out of the room and down the passageway to where the cargo area was, hoping to see the lesser demons that reminded him of his recent hallucinations. Looking at the visual above his hand he guided the remote operating butterfly above head height so that it wouldn't bump into anyone. A few children saw the butterfly and a little girl remarked excitedly to her parents, "Look, mum... Look dad. A butterfly!" She pointed to the fluttering insect above their heads. Then a bird like creature the size of a terrier dog flew up the passageway and engulfed the metallic buttlerfly in a quick decisive movement. "Aw mum, that creature just ate the butterfly."

Zyi was quite stunned that the creature had appeared and wondered where it came from. Tapping the illusions with his finger tips he selected: Energy blast. Strength 1. And fired. The butterfly blasted a hole within the dark brown, furry, flying beast and emerged dripping slime and flew off towards its destination, as the dead corpse of the beast fell to the ground oozing gore. "That's gross," said her mother.

"How strange," said the father.

"At least the butterfly escaped," the little girl's brother told his sister, as she stared horrified at the dead beast on the floor.

"I don't like killing creatures," stated Zyi to Niara who had been watching the visual, "but that gadget is worth over 10,000 credits and there was no way that I was going to catch the creature and force it to vomit to retrieve my expensive piece of equipment; it had to die."

"We are taught at a young age to respect life. There are many things that your world does not know about life after death and reincarnation. When we reach my home planet, you will see." Niara, although disappointed by Zyi's lax attitude towards life forms, knew it had a lot to do with the culture he was brought up in and to a certain degree his innate personality. The butterfly found the storage area, but there was no sign of the demons. He noticed a gaping hole in the ship's wall and there were crew members measuring up the damage. There were also a few people outside soaking up the sun. Niara said, "I can't believe that the lesser demons have escaped. Let's go outside and get some vitamin D3. There's nothing like real sun." They made their way towards the cargo bay and stepped outside into the warm sun after being warned that it was at their personal risk to do so and anything that happened to them would not be covered by their insurance.

The clearing where the ship had landed was not natural. The ship had burnt a disintegrating beam in the area before landing. "There might be a few local herbs here that I can take for analysis," remarked Niara, who also had an interest in herbalism.

"Don't wander off too far. I am just going to sit here and finish off my sandwich." Zyi still held a *Gorno* meat snack in his left hand. The butterfly was hovering in front of him awaiting further instructions.

Niara wandered into the rain forest looking for interesting plants, when she came across a bright blue flower that seemed to emit a high pitched sound, faintly audible, then yellow sparks erupted from the long thin anthers of the plant. She thought that it was a most curious specimen, so she pulled it up by its stem and cast a preservative spell on it so it would stay in a state of suspended animation for the journey back to Dimo. Wandering a bit deeper into the rain forest to see if there were any other interesting flora, she came across several species that were unfamiliar to her. Examining them, she was about to pull one up when a great crashing sound came from deeper within the foliage. Turning, she was taken by surprise by an exceptionally fast, white furred, humanoid giant with the features of a jackal and claws for hands. The giant creature took a swipe at her before she could cast any spells and caught her across the face, sending her to the ground into unconsciousness.

He picked her up and he slung Niara over his shoulder and bounded off through the rain forest back toward his dwelling. Aylisha, the fairy, sensed that something was wrong, lifted the pouch flap around Niara's waist and zipped out to see the white giant lumber off at a swift pace deeper into the rain forest. Drawing her magical rune sword, it emanated a green glow and Aylisha flew super fast and slashed at the giant's hand that held Niara. The beast stopped and turned to face the nimble fairy. A small cut was trickling blood from his hand down onto Niara's clothes. The creature sent Aylisha flying into the undergrowth with a swing of its great arm, slapping into her with its clawed hand. Though the fairy was quick to recover and flew at a quickening speed, trying to blind the giant with a few precise cuts aimed at its eyes, the jackal featured giant let forth a stream of fire, from what looked like a stone embedded in its forehead, which caught Aylisha off guard as she just about managed to deflect some of it, while still catching alight. The fairy fluttered to the ground with serious burns and lay there on fire. A small brown, furry telekin, the size of a tangerine, flickered within the space of several metres, travelling in jumps, as it teleported across the expanse. Tipping a great conical flower filled with water, it poured the contents onto Aylisha extinguishing the flames. The white giant continued towards its destination. With super fast speed it was soon out of the area and deeper into the undergrowth.

Zyi finished his sandwich and proceeded to wipe off the slime, which was still on the butterfly, with a small napkin. Looking around there was no sign of Niara so he stood up and wandered into the forest, the butterfly just ahead. 'Where could she be?' he thought to himself. A small light flickered towards him within the space of a few metres and the small brown telekin stopped in front of him. With a blink of its eye and by turning, it made a motioning movement for Zyi to follow and then flashed off towards some large ferns where there were a collection of large blue flowers. The telekin stopped by the ground and Zyi noticed Aylisha lying there, still breathing and badly burnt, so he picked her up and she slowly stirred. Managing a few words Aylisha spoke; "A big, white monster took Niara. You must find her."

Zyi cursed at this misfortune and set off into the depths of the rain forest looking for signs that he might be able to track the creature with, the telekin teleporting in steps, several metres in front, seeming to know where it was going. Zyi followed. Aylisha was in Zyi's hand and she began to cast healing spells on herself and had soon healed the nasty burns that she had suffered. Zipping out of his hand, Aylisha rested on Zyi's shoulder, sitting there, eyes peeled on the immediate environment ahead, with the rune sword lying across her legs, one hand on the hilt the other on the flat of the blade. The emanation of the runes cast an emerald green glow.

Giz and his fellow lesser demons were deep into the rain forest where they had stumbled across an abandoned wreck of a spacecraft that looked like it had been there for many centuries. It had started to rain, quite heavily. The lesser demons took refuge within the structure of the ruined vessel and, using the remote control dragon, that was a little battered, but still working, the lesser demon with the sparkly sunglasses blasted fire on each of the little demons in turn, to invigorate their skin which was becoming wrinkled, and the fire made them smooth again. The little demon with the long silver cape sighed in relief when he was blasted by the fire breathing metallic dragon and he rolled around a bit on the floor, invigorated. Ratty still had the laser ball cannon and was blasting holes in the rusty metallic walls of the craft for fun. A few more blasts later there were numerous holes in the walls, and wires hung from the gaping wreckage. The great beast with the face of a jackal appeared at the entrance and Ratty stopped firing the laser ball cannon and turned to aim it at the creature who had Niara slung over his shoulder. It paused a moment and then, considering the lesser demons not to be a threat, entered within and went into the complex of passageways that led into the heart of the ship where it had its lair.

Kline and Dia were on the trail of the lesser demons with a small hand-held device which located fine ether matter up to 20km, which also tracked their position. Kline, looking at the reading, said, "There are four signals on the screen just 10km from here, so they are not too far off, we must head northwest."

"They've got quite a head start. I think that we should catch up with them before nightfall though if we keep on the move," Dia said, hoping that they would not miss their flight. Travelling for another hour Kline noticed that the ether readings had not moved, "They're staying still. I wonder why. Maybe they've found something, or they have been captured by the Uto tribes."

"I don't think that the Uto tribes could cope with the little demon with the flaming blue face. He has advanced magic and is quite skillful. I think it would be a bit too much of a plate-full for them," Dia remarked.

Kline smirked at this and said, "Well, I'm sure it would be a shock to their primitive culture if they suddenly got a wave of fire thrown at them!" Kline knew full well what the winged lesser demon was capable of and wondered about whether to abandon it and just get the original three back to earth. The blue-flamed one was a bit of a risk. 'Anyway,' he thought to himself, 'I haven't got the technology to capture it, shame though, it is a unique specimen.'

After another couple of hours of slow hacking with a stick through the undergrowth and the rain, Kline stated,"They're just up ahead," and soon they reached the site of the wrecked carcass of the spacecraft. "That's strange," said Kline, "There are five other readings on the ether monitor. According to it there are other lesser demons about six kilometres north. It might be worth checking out."

Dia frowned at Kline's proposal, "I think we should just get the three and then get back. We don't want to bite off more then we can chew."

"We'll see," Kline said as they made their way towards the entrance of the derelict ship.

There was no sign of the little demons when they entered the wreckage, but they were glad to get out of the pouring rain. Kline noticed several holes in the side of the wall and pointed, saying, "I think Ratty has been having some fun with the laser ball cannon, by the looks of things." Looking at the ether device Kline was aware that the pursued were still in the craft, just a bit further in. Kline motioned to Dia that they were somewhere deeper inside and she followed Kline's lead, both of them soaked to the bone, but they were determined to capture at least three of the lesser demons. Making their way along the interior of the wreck they notice plant life growing where water had gained entry, carrying various seeds of the rain forest with it which had in turn grown into vines and various greenery with some flowers giving off a sweet scent. Upon reaching a doorway where the metal door was corroded and lay on the floor with several insects scurrying over it with bits of dead plant debris, they pass through and turn a corner into a room, where the four little demons were in the act of tearing the head off of a semi-plastic statue of a stately figure that was within an alcove. Giz threw the head in the air and Ratty blasted it with the laser ball cannon, sending it flying across the room in a ball of flaming, melting plastic. "Good shot Ratty!" said Kline to the lesser demon.

They all turned to look at the two humans and Ratty pointed the cannon at him. "There is no need for that sort of attitude," Dia said and then waved her hand, sending the little demon falling backwards onto the floor. Kline threw some acorns at the little demon in the silver cape and it brought up a force field around it, trapping the demon with the sparkly sunglasses as well. Then Giz sent a flurry of small fire balls at Dia which she managed to avoid, apart from one which caught her arm and made a hole in her clothes and burnt some of her skin. Kline then threw the other acorns at Ratty who was just getting up, and the cannon was out of reach when the acorns became active and surrounded him. Giz now faced Kline and the little demon sent a wave of green fire at him. Trying to dive out of the way Kline was unsuccessful and caught the full force of the green fire, knocking him out cold as Dia gave a gasp of disbelief. Dia stood where she was as Giz turned his head in her direction and another wave of green fire went in her direction. As she closed her eyes in fear and acceptance of her fate nothing came, instead she heard Niara's voice. Dia opened her eyes and a shimmering shield was in front of her. Then Niara cast a holding spell on Giz, but he was too quick this time and threw another wave of fire at them whilst zipping out of the room through another exit. Niara bent down to examine Kline and cast some healing spells on him. "Another minute and it would have been too late to save him,"

Niara said as she moved her hand over his eyes and they flicked open.

"What happened?" he asked.

"The winged lesser demon cast a wave of green fire at you and you didn't get out of the way in time," replied Dia.

"Oh, the usual then!" he remarked.

"Doesn't your humour have any ending?" Dia said seriously.

Niara stood up and said, "You're lucky to be alive."

Dia, looking at Niara, said, "How did you get here?"

"Well, I was sort of accosted by a big white hairy beast that left me in a room full of bones and skulls. There was a great boulder blocking the way out, so I blasted it to pieces with a force spell."

Kline, still a bit shaky, walked over to where the lesser demons were trapped and tapped a button on his wrist strap, making the force barriers around them lift and follow him out of the room. Dia and Niara followed and they left the wreckage of the craft to make their way back to *The Mule*, unconcerned about not having captured the other demon with the flaming blue mask. Dia had persuaded him not to pursue the other lesser demons that had shown up on the ether monitor.

Hours seemed to pass as Zyi and company made their way through the dense forest. It had started to rain during the hike and Zyi feared that the great demon would appear after what had happened in the Park of Angels, but there was no recurrence. After a long time following the telekin and stopping sometimes to drink water from the great flowers that held rainwater it started to get dark and they stopped so Zyi could have a convenience pill which would last till the following afternoon. Searching his side pack Zyi's dread mounted when he discovered that he had left the tablets that Niara had given to him for the virus he had on the side table of his room. 'What is going to happen to me?' he thought. The fact that Niara was captive and possibly dead was a concern to him, also he wondered if *The Mule* would wait for them to return, or would they be stranded on a world that they barely knew, with untold dangers?

Gathering some rotted wood from the ground Zyi started to make a fire, which Aylisha set alight with magic and they soon had warmth; it had started to get cold. Looking down at his power boots he noticed some wet earth on them and tried to wipe it off, but it was not soil and he realised that it was a burn that had scorched itself into the electronics. 'Damn,' he thought. Checking the operational system he found out that it was no longer functional. 'It must have been some sort of acid from a plant,' he thought, as the telekin made some musical notes. Trying to communicate with the telekin proved difficult, and Zyi could only just make out its voice as a string of notes that didn't seem to make words but sounded more like music.

Resting his head on a moss mound Zyi covered his eyes with his arm and started thinking about the future, about Dimo and whether he would ever reach it. Slowly drifting off to sleep Zyi started to hear voices. It started as a low dissonant sound and then started to rise in intensity as a string of unfamiliar words, until several lesser demons appeared and were stabbing at him.

He could feel a strong burning pain in his chest and his eyes flicked open to see the darkness above with the faint sound of night creatures. The fire was still burning and he sat upright, his eyes darting from left to right as half formed shapes were moving in his field of vision. The demons soon disappeared and Zyi tried to get some sleep but kept feeling a burning pain in his body and the whispers of a demonic language inside his head. All night he was restless and the fiery pain got worse until it was in his brain. Giving up on trying to get some sleep, he sat by the fire warming his hands and carving entwining knot work into a piece of wood with his laser knife. The demons returned and started to attack him. This made him react with spontaneous movements by covering his body with his arms to stop the ether swords from burning him, but it was not working and to avoid being hurt he ran. Targeting the lesser demons with the butterfly's weapons he blasted energy bolts at them, but all he succeeded in doing was setting some of the trees on fire causing winged creatures to take flight as he continued to unleash the butterfly's weapons in the surrounding area. Aylisha awoke at the noise he was making and followed his trail of destruction with the telekin close behind. Zyi eventually came to a halt when he was too exhausted to run, and, still trying to fend for himself, he writhed on the ground flailing his arms to stop the invisible attacks of the haunting visions of the lesser demons of his imagination. Aylisha tried to calm him down with words, but it seemed that he was not listening, so she cast a musical charm spell which captivated him and he became hypnotized by the effect.

"Lead us back to the ship," Aylisha said to the telekin, hoping that it would understand. The petite life form just blinked in and out of the space between them with a quizzical look on its face. Then Aylisha made an illusion of *The Mule* and pointed at it saying, "Take us there." The telekin then zipped forward in a zig-zag fashion into the forest. Zyi, being under the enchantment of the spell, followed Aylisha and the telekin at the fairy's command. After an hour it started to become light and they reached a site where there were several carved stone figures of forest creatures, standing at over ten feet tall. Aylisha by this point started to doubt that the telekin was leading them in the right direction.

The walk back to *The Mule* was uneventful for Kline, Niara and Dia. Using the ether monitor's tracking device they retraced their steps and arrived at the craft before nightfall. Kline took the lesser demons to his room where he could keep his eye on them and then retired to the social area for some hot food and Dia's company. Whilst eating Niara walked up to Kline's table and asked if he had seen Zyi. "No, not since last night," he replied.
"I've got a feeling that he is in the rain forest looking for me." Niara spoke with uncertainty, knowing that Aylisha was nowhere to be seen. Then an announcement came over the communicator; "We will be resuming our flight shortly now that the repairs have been made. We apologize for any delay." This worried Niara because she couldn't leave Zyi marooned on this planet, she would have to go after him and think of the consequences later. Going to her room Niara packed a few necessities into a bag and then made her way to the exit hatch where she could leave the ship. On the way a man stopped her and introduced himself as Cortz. He informed Niara that Zyi was in the rain forest and that he knew of his exact location because he had been tracking him. Niara soon realized that he was a moth controller and knew that Zyi's rescue was more money orientated than altruistic. Cortz then spoke, saying, "We must inform the officer in charge to wait for us to return with Zyi and maybe they will let us use one of the small speed crafts that are in the flight bay." Agreeing with this course of action they went to the navigation room and informed one of the craft personnel that there was still a passenger missing, lost in the rain forest. They informed them that with the aid of a speed craft they could be back in two hours. After the captain was notified he agreed to send Rycien, a crew member who would take them and could fly a speed craft to search for Zyi.

Giz was now flying through the rain forest with his flaming blue mask when he heard chanting coming from up ahead. Slowing down slightly he could see flickers of fire through the trees up ahead and approached with interest. As he drew nearer Giz could make out humanoid type beings with strange skin that almost reflected the fire light.

The tribe of people were dancing and wore strange garments that were made from the animals of the rain forest. Giz entered into the fire light of the ceremony and then jumped into a fire to warm himself up. A young Uto boy noticed the little demon sitting within the flames and called to one of the adults, who stopped his drumming on a skin drum using bones to make the rhythm sound. The man came over to where the boy pointed and saw Giz obviously enjoying the fire, with his wings flapping a little, wearing a flaming blue mask. The native man, who had markings all over his body in a dried paste, started to signal to some others that there was a lesser demon on the loose. Several men and women came over and surrounded Giz as the majority continued to proceed with the rituals. A tall man with two small rodent skulls dangling from a vine string around his waist and a long stick with a smooth purple rock in place at the top end prodded Giz with it to make him move out of the fire. Giz thought this a bit of an insult and blasted the purple rock into fragments, leaving the stick the man held smouldering.

The man stood back in astonishment and another, not so afraid, grabbed Giz by the neck and in a swift movement lifted him from the fire. The little demon and the native looked in to one another's eyes for a brief moment, then Giz said, "There is no need for that sort of attitude." The man frowned, not knowing the language that the little demon spoke and before the man could do anything else Giz blasted a hole through him, sending gore and blood flying and the body of the man flew back and lay slumped on the ground, lifeless. The others who had witnessed the horror backed away from the little demon, terrified that it had magic, and a woman that was amongst them started to scream at the body of her dead lover which was motionless on the ground. Some of the others who were partaking in the ceremonial rituals stopped their procession and came over to where the commotion was coming from. Giz then started to send balls of fire at random at the tribes folk, burning many and sending some running for their lives. The ritual proceedings were soon halted as people were running around on fire and screaming in agony. The head shaman saw Giz zipping around throwing balls of fire at people and, raising his hands up in the air, the shaman started to cast a spell. Giz saw the shaman with his hands in the air in the middle of summoning greater power to harm him, so Giz sent a flurry of fire daggers in his direction which penetrated the shaman in several places and he fell over and lay bleeding on the ground in a state of intense pain as the fire daggers remained in him, hissing as the blood slowly evaporated with the heat of the fire knives that were protruding from him.

As Giz was wandering around he noticed that there were five blocks of ice on a ledge so he went up to them and noticed that each one contained a little demon. When he came to the block with the demonette from dimension X655 he looked in wonder at her horns and her face, finding her enchanting. With a small wave of fire the ice soon melted and the demonette was still alive and started shivering, so Giz took her hand and flew with her to the nearest fire and they both sat within it. The demonette soon recovered from her ordeal and Giz removed the flaming blue mask; she stared at Giz in bewilderment, for he was the one she was constantly watching in the matrix gap back in dimension X655. She started to speak, but the language was unfamiliar to Giz, but it didn't take him long before he understood that she was letting him know her name, which was Meeky. After Meeky was sufficiently warmed up Giz took her by the hand and replaced the mask to frighten anyone who might try and stop them; he flew into the rain forest with her to get away from the tribe folk who were more scared than interested in him. Eventually, the two ended up on top of a great tree and watched the slow dawn from there, as the sky turned from a deep purple to a hazy gold.

Rycien was in control of the speed craft, with Cortz and Niara as passengers in the back seats. After about half an hour Cortz said that Zyi was down below, probably resting because the moth was not moving, so Rycien slowed the craft to a hover and lowered it down, snapping branches and crushing ferns, until it came to rest. Niara was the first to leave the craft, and she cast a light spell around the area to see where Zyi was, and also Aylisha if she was with him, but there was no sign of them. Cortz found the moth on the ground when he made it glow. "He must have brushed it off somehow," he said.

"That means that he could be absolutely anywhere," replied Niara.

Rycien spoke, saying, "We have got two or three hours to find him, then we must return to *The mule*."

"I don't think that we have that much chance of finding him." Cortz said quite negatively.

"We have a life detector on board the speed craft, though it does not guarantee success it is worth a try," Rycien said, trying to give Niara some hope.

They went back to the craft and set off again on their search for Zyi and Aylisha. The life detector was activated, but they had to fly quite slowly for it to be effective. There were a few false alarms as some big creatures native to the planet were detected and were scared away by the lights of the craft. Time continued to pass as they scoured the forest, then several life forms were noticed, and then about thirty more. "It's more than likely to be one of the tribes that live here," said Rycien. "And time is running out. We will have to turn back."

"Drop me off here," Niara said with determination in her voice.

Rycien replied, "Have you lost your mind? *The mule* is leaving the planet; you will be stranded here."

"I can't leave him. There is too much at stake... Things you do not know."

"Okay then. I will inform the captain about the situation and he will send a rescue party here, which should arrive within the week, so you can be assured that help will be on its way." Rycien had a tone of warmth to his voice as he admired Niara's courage.

Setting the speed craft down near where the life forms were detected Niara left and started to head towards the flickering lights. Rycien and Cortz head back to *The mule*.

CHAPTER 10

The debris on the forest floor cracked and crunched under Niara's feet as she made her way toward the signs of life. As the lights drew closer the sound of percussive drums could be heard more clearly; the rhythm was deep and resounded in the night. The shapes of humanoids could be made out as Niara approached the clearing and their voices were melodious, rising in power and pitch. Stepping in to the clearing there were many of them dancing around great fires that reflected on their skin giving them an orange glow. The Uto people moved in an ancient ancestral movement as if they were one, their arms flailing in different directions, with twirling hand movements, their bodies rising and twisting to the tribal sounds. Niara cautiously walked up to where there were some of the folk sitting near a great beast being roasted over a fire. She sat down beside them and they didn't mind that a stranger from another race was in their midst. Trying to communicate with them with hand gestures and basic words, she knew that they weren't familiar with her language or the others she knew.

Eventually, she managed to understand that they were celebrating the spirits of the night with their dances and songs. The one she had initially conversed with passed her a wooden bowl filled with liquid and motioned for her to drink, but Niara refused because she knew that most tribes in the forested worlds throughout the galaxies used different kinds of drugs that influence the mind and body; thinking that her physiology was different to theirs, who knows what effect it would have. They were blowing powder in to each others eyes, which seemed to be giving them extraordinary abilities, making them rise off the ground slightly, hovering in some kind of trance. The celebrations lasted until dawn and Niara tried some of the cooked beast, for she was hungry. When the first morning rays swept over the shadowed side of Zarkon the Uto tribe's folk began to lie down to sleep. During her time in the night she managed to learn that the head of the tribe, a man with a long bone staff with markings on it and a scarred face, was their chief. Approaching him when he had finished the morning prayers, she spoke to him in her native language and he understood some of it and replied that she was far from home. "I know. I am searching for my friend, he is lost somewhere in this forest."

"I not seen him. We have not many visitors." His accent was shaped by his own use of his native tongue.

"Is there any way you could find where he is?"

"Forest is big. I know not where is he."

"Can you do magic that may be able to find him?" Niara said, feeling that asking seemed futile, but she still had hope.

"I can use teeth to find."

Niara was a bit confused by his reply, but he led her to where there was a bare patch of ground and slipped his hand into his pouch that was secured by a leather string around his waist. Revealing a handful of different shaped teeth in his hand that were painted different colours and unfolding a piece of cloth with lines and circles imprinted upon it, he placed the cloth on the ground and moved his hand in a triangular motion over it three times, then dropped the teeth onto it. Frowning, the chief eventually smiled and then said, "He still be alive. He be at death mountain in three days."

"Death mountain. Where is that?"

"It be a day and a night from here."

"Could you draw me a map?" Niara asked hopefully.

"Yes. But must beware of mountain. There be angry ghost there." The chief strode to where there was a wooden hut and entered. Niara waited outside for a few minutes and when he emerged he held a rough parchment which he passed to her. On it was what looked like a river and a circle within a triangle, within a square. The chief then said, "Follow river. Then, when reach stone square, climb. Then see death mountain. Innio will take to river." With that he walked to where a young boy was curled up next to a dying fire and awoke him. The boy listened to the chief and then took Niara's hand. Niara thanked the chief as they walked away. The boy led her out of the clearing to where the river was to be found.

Zyi stared up at the statues of the unfamiliar creatures carved in stone and Aylisha landed on top of one to rest. There were strange vines hanging from the trees and odd insects were flying about. Without realizing it Aylisha fell asleep and the enchantment spell on Zyi broke. Wandering deeper in to the forest, Zyi seemed to be directed by an inner intuition. Before long the voices were back and the visions of tormenting demons were stabbing at him and laughing demoniacally. Then the great demon, which had appeared in the Park of Angels, rose up out of the fire and raised its clawed hands and an energy flowed from them into Zyi. The great demon was laughing maniacally. The pain was intense as it surged through his body and the lesser demons continued to stab at him. Not able to deal with the pain Zyi ran and ran until he collapsed with exhaustion. Not able to defend himself he clutched his head in agony and screamed, "No! No! Get away!" Then within the darkness of his mind a light formed and a soft gentle sound could be heard among the chaos of the demons' voices. He stopped screaming and his hands became less tense. A brightness filled his mind and words formed that were angelic in origin and had a soothing effect on him. The demonic voices were forced to the background; the greater demon disappeared and he could hear a beautiful voice calling his name... "Zyi. Zyi."

Zyi, just listened to the softness of the sound with the faint stirring of the dissonant demonic voices in the background. Then, the voice said, "Zyi. Open your eyes."

Zyi, thought for a minute and then slowly opened his eyes and before him there was a shimmering apparition of an angel. The brightness of her light was brighter than the white which shone in a circle around him. On the outskirts stood several lesser demons kept at bay from the angel's aura. Her lips moved, but the sound was in his head, "Zyi. I am Resiah." Her soft wings were moving slowly and her feet were just above the ground. "I am from beyond the Celestial realm."

Zyi, wondered at her beauty and then said out loud, "Why is this happening to me?"

The angel's countenance glowed radiantly. "There is a war in the Celestial realm where the demons are fighting the angels. You were a great warrior on the side of God and when you were slain your spirit was sent to Earth to be reborn. There is a great evil at work in the form of a demon lord called Nimordi whom you once slew. He managed to create a weapon with the sole purpose of tracking you and the other princes of light to make you all suffer, especially you. You will not remember because of the veil of forgetfulness. But when demons descend from heaven they still have their memories. And it was a long time ago. He will not stop until you are dead, but he wants to make it slow. God knew that this would happen and there are many pathways in your life, some lead to death and others will lead you to destroy the demon lord and the virus he created."

"How will I find him? How can I destroy the virus?"

"These answers are in the future. Just follow your path and the light of goodness will guide you." The angel smiled and raised her hands, disappearing as the lesser demons vaporised into thin air. The last words of the angel sounded; "I will return." Zyi closed his eyes and there was no pain. When Zyi lifted his eyelids he saw the telekin blinking in and out of the space in front of him and there were no demons around. "Where did you come from?" asked Zyi to the telekin. Its reply was a series of musical notes, which Zyi could not interpret to make any sense. The telekin had a clump of small purple berries in its mouth and then looked up blinking. Zyi noticed overhead a tall tree where there were bunches of the berries hanging from the branches. Climbing the tree he was bitten a few times by small insects that were marching up and down it. After acquiring some of the fruit Zyi proceeded to eat. The fruit was sweet and watery, which took away his thirst. Then he wondered where Aylisha was. It would be futile to try and find her in this great expanse of forest; maybe they would come across each other in the next few days, or she would find her way safely back to the ship.

The lesser demon and the demonette descended from the tree tops once the sun was ascending the sky and began to make their way through the forest. Giz stopped suddenly as he noticed a strange creature coming towards them. Meeky also stopped and wondered what the hairy beast was. The animal grunted, it had horns on its head and a twisted snout. Meeky let out a squeal of laughter and jumped on its back. It tried to fling her off but with no success, and bolted into the undergrowth. Giz followed and flew down on the beast's back behind Meeky. The creature began to trample its way through the rain forest at quite a pace, and the two lesser demons rode on the back of it until it ran out of strength and knelt down by a crop of fungi to feast upon them. Meeky was amused by the beast feeding and wondered what it was doing. When it had finished the hairy creature walked on and stopped by a puddle to drink. Meeky saw her reflection in the water and leaned closer to look. As she looked at the red reflection she slipped off the beast and fell head first into the water. Letting out a screech of shock with mild pain, Meeky picked herself up and mounted the beast once again. Giz let out a chuckle and then smiled. Meeky flicked a drop of water in his eye with an unsatisfied look in her expression and he immediately wiped the smile from his face. They continued to ride the beast for most of the day until they came across a great fruit tree where a native of the forest was sitting on the ground underneath it eating. He saw them and immediately picked up his spear and began to chase them, hoping to catch the beast for cooking. After a few minutes of running the man threw his spear and it went wide, narrowly missing its target. T he man then tripped over a root of an old tree and fell face first onto an insect nest and ran off in the other direction screaming as the deadly insects bit into his face. Meeky and Giz turned as the beast kept running and both laughed at the man's distress.

Aylisha awoke and suddenly realized that Zyi was not around. Flying around the statues she couldn't see any traces of where he might have gone so she decided to fly above the treetops to see if there were any landmarks. Once up in the sky, she could see in the distance a mountain looming high. Something made her want to go to the mountain. Something was calling to her, beckoning. Aylisha snapped her eyelids shut and opened them again. Then she zoomed off towards the mountain. She felt that she would find Zyi there, or maybe Niara, if it had the same effect on them.

As the day became longer Zyi began to have different experiences that were not ordinary. He had continuous whispers in his head that were demonic, but they were not very dominant. The trees seemed to have a different light about them as if they were more than just trees. Slowly, Zyi walked up to a great tree that had twisting branches reaching up to the canopy and smooth bark that glistened as some sticky substance was trickling down it from a wound where a bird had caused damage to taste the sap. Laying his hand upon it he felt a slight vibration and memories of pain entered his being as the tree's spirit flooded his body. Zyi withdrew in horror and fell to his knees with the experience. The memory of the tree spanned hundreds of years and in just a few moments Zyi had a glimpse of what the past was like for it. A knowledge came with the shock. A knowledge that this tree was more than just something that grew in the forest. It was a life form and had feelings. It had a memory. A memory that was locked within it, and no one could access it because of its nature. Zyi felt that it had a spirit. A spirit which made it unique and had some past. A past that Zyi just had a fleeting glimpse of. Bewildered and still kneeling, Zyi reached out his hand and placed it once again on the tree. There was a flow of energy which went into Zyi, slow at first, then a steady stream of consciousness. More memories came to Zyi. He understood that the tree was unable to speak in words but it communicated with emotions, and he realised the tree was imparting some kindness towards him as if the soul of the tree had been someone or something he had known before. Then a word came to his mind, it came from the deepest part of his soul and the word was Ejeo. This seemed familiar to him in an odd way. He had never heard the word before but there was something about the sound of it in his head that seemed a part of him, a part of his past, a past that he no longer remembered. Zyi withdrew his hand and stood up. A trace of the tree's spirit flickered pinky-blue and Zyi now knew that life was something deeper than appearances.

Ambling along as a slow pace the telekin flitted in the space in front of him signalling some sort of message that he thought of as a language. Zyi made sense of this and started to wave his hand in the air as he walked while speaking to the telekin, trying to communicate. He took the telekin's movements to be speech and knew them to be some of the history of its race. The telekin made musical notes as well but could not comprehend the language Zyi spoke, but with the motions of his hands had a grasp of what Zyi was trying to convey. This went on for a few hours until Zyi and the telekin reached an enormous plant that was hanging from the trees and seemed to be bearing some sort of fruit. The telekin began to eat from it and Zyi followed its example, knowing that it was not poisonous. It tasted quite sour but was refreshing and they both ate their fill. Then the whispering in his head got louder and the demons were chanting some sort of demonic curse. Zyi started to feel a burning in his chest and it was spreading. Fearing the worst he immediately started to look around, and several lesser demons were standing there, some with ether swords and sly smiles on their faces. They all jumped on him at once and the pain intensified as they only wanted to make him suffer; inside his head he could hear the demon lord laughing.

Niara reached the river and the young boy Innio went back to the settlement. Following the fast moving waters Niara felt confident in the trust she had for the knowledge the chief had imparted to her. Many hours passed and strange birds were diving in the water and emerging with silvery fishes. There were some great beasts that lurked near the water's edge which Niara avoided because they had rows of teeth, looking like a cross between an alligator and a hippopotamus. Within time she reached the stone monument of the three symbols that were drawn on her map. Levitating up, she rested on one of the branches of a gnarled tree and peered ahead to where in the distance could be seen death mountain rising above the horizon of trees. It didn't look that far away but Niara knew that the distance towards the mountain would take several hours to walk, especially through dense forest, so she decided to fly. Soaring through the air, the wind rippling her clothes, she headed towards the mountain. When it was close she descended from the sky and landed near a patch of pink flowers that emitted an intoxicating scent, which reminded her of her mother's perfume. The mountain was high and the summit was covered with snow. It seemed strange because it was hot at ground level. A flicker of orange flitted in her field of vision and she looked to where it had been, but there were rocks there. 'The angry ghost,' she thought to herself, 'I wonder if that was it.' Then she noticed an entrance in the mountain, some way up, which looked like a cave. The heat was quite overwhelming and the cool dark interior of the cave was enticing, so she began to walk towards the entrance she had espied. As she began to climb her way up a fair sized rock skimmed past her head and clattered on the ground. She turned around and saw a fleeting glimpse of orange that darted behind some rocks. 'I think that's the angry ghost,' she thought to herself, and then said out loud, "Show yourself," but there was no reply. Ignoring the threat, she continued to climb, until after several minutes a small rock hit her leg causing pain and she turned around in anger to see the orange ghost floating in the air with another rock in its hand.

"Get off my mountain," it said with a hissing voice.

"Why should I? It's not your mountain."

"Yes it is. You don't belong here. I have lived here for over a thousand years."

"And this is what you do to strangers? Throw stones at them?"

"It's the only way to let them know that they are not welcome."

"You must be a lonely ghost that hasn't many friends if you treat people like that."

"I don't need friends." The ghost looked unhappy and then angry, it raised its arm to throw the rock at Niara. Niara was quick and made a force shield which deflected the assault. The angry ghost continued to throw rocks at her but with no success. Getting tired of defending herself, Niara let off a blast of energy which hurt the ghost and made it cry. Niara felt sorry for it, but it was getting angrier and picked up a huge boulder twice its own size and hurled it at her. The magical defense she created was strong enough to stop the attack and in retaliation she blasted the ghost with a stream of energy which held it in pain. Niara would not stop the flow until the ghost promised to stop throwing rocks.

"No! I am going to crush you," the ghost said, refusing to submit to her demands. The angry ghost was in pain with the stream of energy Niara was directing at it until a blue light shone from the cave up ahead and broke her spell and held the ghost in a trance. A man came gliding down from the mountain and when close enough said, "You shouldn't have hurt the ghost, it will only make her angrier."

"I didn't have much choice. It would have killed me if it had the chance."

"There are ways to deal with angry ghosts. You know magic. I am surprised you do not know."

"I have never had the displeasure of meeting one before," Niara replied. The ghost looked calm and the strange man, with jet black skin, turned the ghost green and it dropped a rock it had in its hand and apologized for being angry.

"It's not your fault," said the man, "You are made like that."

"Well at least it's not angry any more," Niara said as the ghost wandered off, floating, looking quite sad.

The man also looked sad and said, "It will not last long. My magic has its limits."

"So, what are you doing here?" asked Niara and then, realizing that the man was a Jesini, stood in awe.

"I am here for the remainder of my life to teach anyone who wants to learn."

"It's an honour to meet a Jesini," replied Niara, who had a deep respect for the race, a race that is so passive they will never kill anything and if one dies they all die together and reincarnate somewhere else in the universe. Their main aim in life is to convert others to their kind and join them in the life and death of material nature.

"The honour is mine," he replied and then continued, "There are things you do not know. I summoned you here, and you are here for a reason."

Niara was confused at his words and said, "I thought that I am here because fate led me in this direction and it is by chance that we meet."

The jesini smiled and said, "There are many things that you don't understand. There is no such thing as chance. It is all meticulously planned out, but you can change your future. Let us go to my dwelling, up there," he pointed up to a cave entrance, "and we will discuss things further. I have food there. I know that you are hungry and tired."

They both walked up the mountain towards the dwelling as the ghost hovered around in its sadness. Once inside the cave Niara sat down on a floor covering of soft tree bark. The jesini went to the back of the cave and soon returned with a thick leaf which held various fruits of the forest and a strange looking brown stringy strip. "Here, eat this Niara."

"How did you know my name?"

"I know many things. I have met you before, but you will not remember."

"So, what is your name?" Niara asked.

"You can call me Urilon."

Niara started to chew on the brown strip and it tasted surprisingly good. "Why did you summon me here?" she asked.

"It is written that the chosen seven will bring the downfall of a great evil. I cannot explain everything now, but there are things that you need to know. Things that will help in the future."

"Like what?" she enquired.

"We must wait for the other six before I tell you. There are some things that I need to know before I give you information concerning your future. Things that I will only know when the seven of you are together."

"You are expecting more people to come?"

"Yes. They will be here within four days," Urilon said with certainty.

"Zyi, will he be one of them?"

"Yes. But he has changed."

"Changed... He has not been taking his medicine. Maybe he left it back at *The Mule*."

"Yes. But you must realize that sometimes when you are trying to help it is not the best thing. He needed time on his own. There are powers at work here that you do not understand and sometimes what you think is a bad thing can be a blessing."

"I was taught that you have to treat the illness, otherwise it will cause unbearable torment and suffering." Niara was sure that her mentors were knowledgeable in the field of diseases and afflictions.

"There will be a time when it is necessary for him to agree to your prescription, but it must be his choice. Otherwise he will never

know the spiritual nature that he fights for."
"There is an aspect of the DNA weapon that will cause him to hurt himself. I cannot let him get that far down that road of pain." Niara was beginning to doubt Urilon's wisdom.
"I know of the weapon, but it is not as effective here on Zarkon. I have neutralised the weapon in the atmosphere and he is safer here than on Earth."
"I hope you are right."
"Have faith. There is more to a Jesini than most people know."
Niara finished her food and then said, "Is Aylisha one of the seven?"
"Yes," Urilon replied. "She is safe."
Laying her head down on the soft bark, she closed her eyes and mumbled, "I just need some dream time."
Urilon walked out of the cave and cast a spell to shield the cave entrance from the cool breeze that had begun to stir, so as to let Niara have a warm sleep.

Zyi opened his eyes; it was dark, and colours seemed to swirl about the night. The telekin's light blinked in and out of the darkness.
"So, you're still here then," Zyi remarked to the telekin.
The telekin replied with a few musical notes and Zyi said, "What happened? I remember the lesser demons, then I ran and now I wake up." A few more notes from the telekin and Zyi understood that he had fallen and blacked out with too much pain. The whispers were still there which made him slightly uncomfortable but there was no pain. 'When will this ever end?' he thought to himself, 'It's so draining.'

Zyi wandered the night through the forest listening to the sounds of the creatures. A pair of luminous eyes stared at him from the undergrowth which made Zyi stop in his tracks. Staring back at the pale green eyes, Zyi used the illusions on his mini-comp and light shot out in a white square from a point in his wrist. The creature was fully exposed to the brightness and Zyi could see that it was a strange animal that had thick striped fur with a long tail. It froze in the light and then bolted. Zyi thought the creature was more scared of him than was necessary, but after all fear kept it alive and safe from predators. The telekin flitted around in the space around the trees and made musical notes in the process. The demons' voices were in the background and he knew it was a matter of time before they emerged to torment him. After what seemed like a long time wandering in the forest, with the illumination of the mini-comp, there came the sound of voices up ahead. The language was unfamiliar to Zyi and he brightened the light so it lit up more of the forest, and he started to run towards the sound in the hope of some human contact that could help him. Soon, three figures came in view. Two were Natarkian and one was an Uto. Zyi realized at once that this was a bad situation because the Natarkian race hunted the Utos for the pleasure of eating them. The Natarkians had the lone Uto by a length of cord that was bound around his wrists. The Natarkians were speaking in their native dialect and both pointed a weapon at Zyi as soon as he was seen. Zyi released the butterfly and it flew up above them. Using the built in visual display in his left eye and operating the illusions he selected a weapon with a pin point accuracy for sniping. One of the Natarkians spoke in a gruff voice saying, "Who are you?"

"Zyi," he replied and then said, "You know slavery is against galactic law. It is a crime to imprison or capture someone in this day and age." He tried to sound as non threatening as possible, in the hope that they would comply with no resistance.

"It is none of your business. Let us pass," the Natarkian demanded.

"I'm sorry but I don't like to see an injustice being done." Zyi had his aim on the speaker and was ready with the illusions at his fingertips, if things should suddenly go awry.

"Then you shall die!" The Natarkian was quicker than Zyi anticipated and let off a shot from his blaster which went past Zyi into the undergrowth. Within seconds Zyi had tapped the illusion, sending a pin sized high energy shot at the Natarkian. He fell to the ground stunned and unable to move. The other Natarkian looked about for another enemy, for Zyi held no weapon. "Let him go," demanded Zyi.

"It is not our way to avoid combat. We are not cowards!" The remaining Natarkian reached for his gun which was tucked in his belt. Zyi had already targeted the Natarkian and fired, giving his quarry no chance to retaliate. The shot hit its target and the Natarkian fell to the ground paralysed. The remaining Uto started to speak in his native tongue, which Zyi could not grasp, but knew that he was grateful for his freedom. Zyi then cut the bonds around the Uto with his laser knife, and without saying another word the Uto rushed off into the forest to warn his kinsfolk of the danger of hunters.

CHAPTER 11

Niara awoke to the thundering sound of a space craft, flying low, overhead. Getting up from the soft floor covering she stepped outside through the thin transparent barrier that kept the cool air out. Flying over the forest was a bulky space vessel that looked like it was being flown by an amateur. It swerved and dipped in a sketchy manner until it was out of sight. Urilon could be seen coming up the mountain, and when he drew closer she noticed Aylisha was with him. When they reached the entrance to the cave Niara gave Aylisha a warm smile and said, "I knew you would be here soon."

"I felt a strong inclination to come here and my instinct was right," Aylisha replied.

"We should be seeing Zyi soon, and some others," Niara said with some hint of mystery.

"Some others?"

"Yes. We are expecting company." Niara still wondered who they could be but was too glad to see Aylisha to worry too much about who these strangers were.

"Come. There is still some food left if you're hungry," Urilon said, motioning Aylisha to go inside the cave. Aylisha zipped in and found some berries and nuts that she began to eat heartily.

"What was that craft that flew overhead?" Niara asked Urilon.

"Natarkians," came the reply. "They visit here from time to time to take the Uto people. They eat them and use them for slavery."

"That's terrible," said Niara, forgetting the savagery of some of the worlds in this galaxy.

"Yes," replied Urilon, and continued, saying, "Their feud has been going on for thousands of years and the relations between them is bitter."

"Is there no end to war?" enquired Niara in a dismissive gesture.

"You know as well as I that war has been a part of survival ever since the beginning of life in this universe."

"Yes, but it seems so unnecessary. Pointless dying and suffering, especially for those who want no part in it, " Niara spoke with a sharp edge to her voice, knowing full well that she was one of those that opposed war and would gladly give anything for peace.

"Let us go inside and talk further of things. It is approaching sunset and the nights here are cold," Urilon said as he walked towards the cave, and Niara followed.

Zyi walked until the light began to dim and the sun was setting, with only the telekin's musical notes to accompany him on his lonely quest. The telekin had been leading the way and Zyi felt that they must have covered a lot of ground over the hours, then without warning the whispering voices in his mind began to stir and the voices grew louder until the hallucinations began to appear and soon lesser demons were tormenting him with what seemed like voices of fire and they were soon stabbing him with their ether swords. Not being able to stand it for much longer Zyi broke into a run through the underbrush as some of the plant life that had thorns and spikes cut in to his legs and body.

Eventually, he came to a halt and knelt on the forest floor breathing in deep breaths as the little demons surrounded him. Their chanting grew louder and he felt for his laser knife, found it, and switched it on, holding it close to his wrist. Zyi's mind was in anguish with the pain of fire and instinctively the knife cut into his flesh and he dropped it. The cut was clean and the pain was brief, but it was not of his doing and he soon realized that the evil demons were making him suffer in any which way they could. In response to this unforeseen danger and in a moment of clarity Zyi picked up the laser knife and threw it out into the foliage of the forest, thinking that it was better lost than a threat in the future when the demons had taken over. Collapsing onto the ground Zyi lay there in shock as the whispering faded and the demons disappeared. The telekin was beside him and was making musical notes. "I know, but I am scared" said Zyi. "You can't see them, but they are real. The little demons."

The telekin responded with a few beeps.

"You can see them too?" Zyi asked.

The telekin answered in its usual musical fashion, in acknowledgement.

"Well, thanks for staying with me. If it wasn't for you I would have no one to talk to." Zyi then thought that the creature must have a name and asked.

The telekin made a sound that Zyi interpreted as *Muox*. "Thank you Muox. My name is Zyi. Nice to meet you."

"Beep bleep, hum."

"So, where are you leading me, in this vast forest?"

The telekin answered and Zyi replied, "Who is Urilon?"

"Bleep bleep, beep."

"A great sage from a race that was one of the first born in the universe who has valuable knowledge for me. Well, I haven't got much time to see him. I need to find Niara. She is the only one that can help me."

"Beep, bleep hum bleep."

"She will be there? Are you sure?"

"Beep."

"We'd better be on our way then. Is it far?"

"Bleep."

Zyi picked himself up off of the ground and wiped free some of the debris that clung to him. "Lead the way Muox."

Urilon sat upon a soft leaf covered floor in a niche in the cave. Three small balls of fire were suspended in the space above, giving off enough illumination so that they could see each others' faces clearly. Aylisha picked up one of the soft furry leaves and flew up to a natural jut that protruded from the stone, near one of the fire balls, and proceeded to sit there on the leaf warming her hands near the magical fire.

"It has been a while since I've had company," said Urilon.

"It must get lonely living in isolation here on Zarkon, with no other humans or Jesinis." Niara wondered how he coped without the familiar comfort of companionship.

"I do not get lonely. Us Jesinis are bonded by flesh and thought. Whatever one thinks, the others know. So, I am in essence never alone."

"How can you hear the thoughts of all your kindred? It must be confusing." Niara asked, her curiosity aroused.

"Well, it is like seeing shapes, sounds and colours all blended into one. They are distinguishable and I know each of them by name and appearance. They are my brothers and sisters who have become Jesinis by the very nature of their souls."

"Is it true that if one Jesini dies, you all die?" Niara said, hoping that her question was not thought of as prying into the nature and secrets of a race that was known on Dimo as peaceful and was honoured and respected.

"It is true, yes. It is a natural occurrence and it is what we are gifted with. For us to remain in one consciousness we all pass away together to be reborn somewhere else in the universe, to live and guide the lost and to teach the mysteries of nature and God." Urilon made an illusion of a grasshopper, which had a faint blue aura, then it jumped into the air and transformed itself into a bird the size of an insect. It flew around the cave leaving a trail of misty lights, before disappearing in a flash. Niara smiled and said, "So, who have you met here, to teach the knowledge you know?"

"You are the first." Urilon paused, then continued, "And the last."

"You mean that your whole existence here is to teach me and Zyi?"

"Yes; it is of no little consequence. When a stone is dropped into water it creates ripples. From small things great deeds are done, and my life is always worth living, even if it means waiting for a thousand years to impart knowledge that takes a few moments to pass on. I am here to serve."

"I have heard much of the humble Jesini, who would rather die than kill. Your race is indeed one which is inspiring. A lot of people, from all civilizations across the galaxies, draw close to your way of life in the spiritual paths which unfolds before them," Niara was filled with admiration at the thought of being honoured by this great being, whose sole purpose for existence was to guide and serve. She and Zyi were the purpose of his life; she was almost tearful at the fact that someone she didn't even know that well considered her worth waiting for, and was alive for no other reason than to serve. Niara spoke in a calm voice; "What am I here to learn?"

"There is not much that I am going to tell you, but what I do say will have its repercussions. We must first wait for your friend. He will be here tomorrow and he has been through a lot, so he needs time to heal."

It was now dark and Urilon brought a handful of sweet nuts with three different fruits he had gathered earlier from the forest, and said, "This will suffice for now. The fruit is quite filling and the nuts are good for health."

Aylisha flew down from her ledge, where she had been listening intently, and picked up one of the nuts, "Mmm, they taste like *hanir*, from my home world." She began to eat her fill and Urilon went into the back of the cave and returned with a metal bowl which contained a milky liquid, "This is vine milk and is good for you, please drink, it is quite refreshing." Urilon gestured to Niara and she held the bowl to her lips and drank.

The night wore on and after more talk Urilon said, "You must be tired now. I will let you sleep." He returned with a soft downy blanket made of an assortment of feathers, "Here, this will keep you warm."

Niara, snuggled up in the blanket and wrapped it about herself, with her thoughts on Zyi and what he must have gone through these last few days since they left *The Mule.*

Morning light flooded into the cave and Niara awoke gazing up at the three fire balls that had been burning through the night. She arose and realized she was alone. Stepping outside, the breeze was refreshing and she noticed the ghost floating around near the forest edge at the base of the mountain. Aylisha came flying up with a purple flower in her hand, and spoke; "There are so many wild flowers I have never seen in the forest. We must collect some seeds to take back with us."

"That's a good idea. I'm sure my mother would love to grow some exotic flowers from this galaxy," Niara said eagerly. The two of them went into the fringes of the forest looking for seed pods. Niara collected some plants with roots which she wrapped in thick waxy leaves, filling them with soil and stitching them together with strands of vine.

It was soon afternoon and the sun was in the clear sky. Urilon saw Niara and Aylisha ascend the mountain slope and the angry ghost was nowhere to be seen. When the two reached the cave entrance Urilon said, "I have prepared some food."

Niara, could smell freshly cooked vegetables, and Urilon presented a wooden plate with several fried pieces of roots and succulent leaves with chunks of carbohydrates. A thick sauce of ground seeds mixed with sap and honey complimented the dish. Niara ate with a healthy appetite and when she finished she thanked Urilon and said, "Are you not eating?"

"I don't eat, " he replied. "The only sustenance I need is air and sunlight."

"You don't know what you're missing," she replied. "Where did you learn to cook so well?"

"My memories go back a long way Niara, and not just my memories."

There was the sound of an explosion outside and Aylisha darted into the air, startled. "What's that?" she said.

"I think your friend is here," Urilon answered.

"Zyi?" Niara replied.

"Yes. I think he's encountered the angry ghost," Urilon remarked in a knowing tone.

Aylisha, was the first out of the cave, zipping through the air and up a little bit to peer down at Zyi who was arguing with the ghost. Niara as soon as she saw Zyi, was elated to see him alive. "Zyi," she called out. He looked up and a wide grin spread upon his face. "Niara. I've found you at last!" Then he turned to the ghost and said, "It is not your mountain. I can go where ever I choose and you're not going to stop me. No wonder you haven't any friends."

The angry ghost picked up another rock and said somewhat sulkily, "I don't need friends, and if you don't get off my mountain I will throw this at you." The ghost threw the fair-sized stone up in the air a few times, catching it in his hand. Urilon watched as Zyi blasted the rock in mid-air with the butterfly's weapon, as the ghost was throwing and catching it.

The fragments of rock scattered in the explosion, leaving a cloud of dust that dispersed in the breeze, and the ghost was left empty handed. Zyi then proceeded to climb up towards Niara and the ghost decided to let him pass because Zyi was an interesting human who made things disappear with a loud bang.

After a brief climb, Niara stood there and took Zyi's arm, leading him into the cave, so they could sit and talk, as the breeze was turning cooler. Inside, Muox the telekin spotted some of the sweet nuts and took one between his teeth and began to chew. Niara was in a good mood and was overjoyed to have Zyi in her company again. They sat for a few moments in silence, then Niara noticed the gashes on Zyi's arm where he had harmed himself. "What happpened to your wrist?" she asked.

"Oh, I used the laser knife on myself when the demons were tormenting me."

"I was worried that something like that would happen. You are lucky to still be alive," Niara said, frowning.

"I think the demon lord enjoys it more if I suffer. I think that is why I'm still here. It must give him pleasure to torment me."

"I know. The demons are like that. Now you know that what you are infected with is very serious. Your only chance for treatment is on Dimo. There, we can destroy the virus and guard you against further infection" Niara said, trying to give Zyi some hope.

"How long do you think it will take for us to reach your home world?"

"Well, if all goes well and we get off this planet within a week, it shouldn't take longer than twelve days."

Changing the subject, Zyi said, "The virus isn't all bad. I've had some interesting experiences. I can sense energy in trees. I'm sure they are alive in a way we do not understand."

"Where I come from there is evidence that there is life in all things and that material objects have a sort of memory, a kind of soul. What you see is known as the life force, that all things have.

Zyi thought about the apparition of the angel Resiah, but didn't feel like talking about it. In a way he did not know what Niara would make of that experience, though Niara was open minded about these things, and also she believed in God, which meant that she would understand, he was sure, but it was kind of personal and he decided he would talk of it at a later time.

"Let me take a look at your arm." Niara pulled the sleeve up so that the burn marks from the laser knife showed. The seared skin was a shiny red and looked sore. "Does it still hurt?" she asked.

"No, the pain was brief and I threw away the knife so it couldn't happen again."

Niara, moved her fingers over the marking with a soft feathery touch. A cool sensation emanated from her fingertips and Zyi felt soothed by it as she moved in small circles, massaging the tender skin. The sensitive skin started to heal and the swelling soon turned back to its original colour.

"That's better," she said.

Urilon, soon appeared with a cone shaped flower filled with water and passed it to Zyi, saying, "You must be thirsty."

Zyi said, "Thank you."

Niara thought about how Zyi might in the course of the next few days be without medicine. Standing up, she approached Urilon who was at the far end of the cave preparing some food, under a yellow burning ball of fire, so he could see.

"Urilon, you must know this forest well enough to find some ingredients to make a medicinal powder or drink for Zyi? I fear that he might slip into harming himself again."

"I know your fears and I have the substances here." He passed Niara a small woven bag with flower petals, roots, fungi and berries within. "That is all you need," he said.

Aylisha flew over to Zyi, who was still holding the water filled flower and she said, "Can I have a sip?" Zyi held out the water vessel before her and she flitted her wings like a humming bird, cupping her hands, bringing up water which she steadily drank from. Then she flew to where the telekin was watching Urilon making a fire, where a metal tray hung suspended over it. The tray was porous and Urilon said to Aylisha "The tinder I am using is from a scented tree, which adds fragrance to the food when the smoke rises up through the holes in the metal tray." The telekin blinked over at the food that was frying and blinked away again with a thick fleshy root in its mouth, unable to wait for the food to cook through thoroughly. Aylisha laughed at this, for it seemed like the furry telekin must have thought that Urilon would not share the sustenance with it. Within a few minutes the telekin was back in the cave for more.

After eating, Niara began telling Zyi what had happened when she was accosted by the beast in the forest. Urilon sat down on an assortment of thick leaves and they were all engaged in conversation until late in the night, about different worlds where you would be sentenced to death for smoking, and about the world called Wali where the seas and rivers were orange. Niara busied herself preparing the medicine for Zyi by mixing them together and heating them up to break down the compounds into a paste. Urilon was listening to Zyi talking about his life and how he had lost his parents in the garden of Zyprus and how he had grown up in the care of a youth home that catered for the needs of children who had no family. Zyi had learned to dismantle machines and reconstruct them with great care at the age of nine. He had studied electronics and became a pilot of a small space faring craft that shipped materials to other planets, before his career move to self-employment, doing jobs for organizations to recover information that should otherwise have remained hidden. This line of work proved quite fruitful in the way of payment and he was soon learning to avoid the justice agents, who after a short period of time were on his trail after a series of explosions in an underground complex. Urilon sat and listened until Zyi mentioned the incident at the Park of Angels, where the great demon lord Nimordi crossed through and came into the world of mortals.

"It takes a lot of magic power to enter our realms and with a host of lesser demons it is no easy endeavour." Urilon knew that the demon lord must be very powerful. "It may be the case that Nimordi has a personal vendetta against you, to go to all that trouble to enter our realm and not to slay you. It seems he has a reason to make you suffer, which may be connected to your life in the celestial realm." Urilon paused for thought.

Aylisha flew over to Niara and watched her stirring the ingredients.

A sweet vapour rose up from the metal dish. "Will that keep the demons away?" she asked.

"It will have that desired effect, but it will not stop the burning pain," Niara clarified.

"Well, that should help," Aylisha responded with sympathy.

Zyi began hearing the whispering voices in his head and feared that the demons would soon appear.

"It is late. You must all rest." Urilon had sensed the drowsiness in Niara's voice as she said to herself in a half-whisper that she had finished. "It won't be ready till the morning," she said, picking up the metal dish and leaving it near the side. "It has to cool down for a few hours."

A bundle of fine cotton was heaped up near the cave entrance, which Urilon had gathered earlier from the nest of a winged rodent who had acquired it from a native animal that had shed its winter coat for this time of year when the weather was warmer. Making another soft floor covering for Zyi with the same soft furry leaves, Urilon wished them good night and left the cave. Niara fell asleep immediately and Aylisha rested on a mound of cotton, where the telekin had dug itself in. Zyi lay under a downy blanket and the whisperings of demonic voices were steadily and inevitably getting louder. A red skinned lesser demon appeared under one of the balls of fire and pointed at Zyi with its ether sword. Zyi watched as it darted towards him and, expecting pain, he closed his eyes, but none came. Instead a shining light the size of a little star shone in his mind, and a beautiful voice sounded; "I have returned," Resiah said. "There will be no more demons tonight."

Zyi than felt as if a burning sun was aflame in his heart and he felt bliss, which was like a rush of photons invading the darkness of his soul.

"I am your guardian angel," she said with a tenderness in her voice. "One day you will be here in life immortal, and that day will come."

Zyi felt as if other memories were filtering through from the depths of his unconsciousness, memories of another life, a life in the celestial realm, where he had seen her before and her aura was more shining than the other angels that were there because she had come from heaven, with some of the other high angels that were there that had the same brightness. The image of Resiah settled on his mind and he could see how beautiful she was, coming from the highest spiritual realm.

The hours passed and Zyi eventually fell asleep to the sound of Resiah's voice, as the words turned from speech to a soft harmonious melody.

Niara was the first to awake to the sound of what was like a strange animal with hiccups. Urilon, noticing that she had awoken said, "The others are here."
"The others? You mean the other chosen ones?"
"Yes."
Niara arose and walked to the edge of the cave and was not expecting to see two lesser demons, one with a flaming blue mask and the other with horns, at the edge of the mountain. The strange sound came from the ghost who was laughing at the little demons.

CHAPTER 12

Niara turned to Urilon in bewilderment and said, "Surely these little demons are not going to be our companions?"
"There is more to them than just appearances Niara," he replied.

The two lesser demons came up the rocky mountain. Giz was still wearing the flaming blue mask which flicked serpentine tongues of light. The angry ghost trailed behind them, unable to control its mirth. When Giz and Meeky were within three metres of Urilon, Giz bowed in respect and Meeky responded also with a low bow. Urilon spoke to Giz in an ancient dialect which the lesser demon understood and the Jesini motioned for them all to enter the cave.
Zyi was just waking up and flinched when he saw the two little demons walking in through the cave entrance. Giz offered his hand in greeting and Zyi took the small demon's hand to shake which felt hot so he had to let go quickly as it was burning him. Giz smiled as if he knew Zyi from another life.
Aylisha couldn't believe that the two lesser demons were going to be able to help them on their journey to Dimo.
"You will not be going to Dimo just yet. There are other things you must do before you reach that destination. There are more lives to consider than just your own." Urilon knew that Aylisha and Niara would disagree.
"What do you mean?" Niara said with astonishment. "We must get to my home world to destroy the virus that is active in Zyi. There is no other alternative."
Urilon recognised the urgency of Niara's plea but he had other information that demanded imperative attention. "I'm afraid that the virus has reached other galaxies that were meant to stay unaffected, where souls have reincarnated from the celestial realm in a great number. Because of their limited technology and medicine they are vunerable to its effects. Many people are dying and suffering the weapon's violent nature, which leaves us no other course of action to consider other than to destroy the mirror of souls."
"The mirror of souls?" Zyi enquired.
"Yes. The demon lord Nimordi has the mirror within his dimension. With magic and the technology of advanced engineering, this artefact is the link from the ether dimension to the mortal universe. It can be used to discriminate individuals for suffering. Once

destroyed it will leave the virus ineffective. It is the main power source which allows the virus to operate." Urilon knew that the mirror had to be destroyed and that the chosen seven were to fulfill the prophecy.

"How are we supposed to find this dimension? There are countless realms of demons going in to the hundreds of thousands that haven't been mapped." Niara knew about this from her home planet Dimo, from one of her friends who was researching dimensions.

"There is a way. These little demons can assist." Urilon glanced over to Giz and Meeky.

"The lesser demons? How can they help?" Niara asked.

"All will be revealed in time," Urilon replied mysteriously.

Giz, nodded in agreement and said, "There is more to these little demons than just appearances. All will be revealed." Giz waved his ether sword in Niara's direction.

Aylisha and Zyi laughed. "He is quick at picking up our language," Zyi remarked.

Urilon spoke up and said, "It will soon be time for you to leave this planet. The rescue team are here and are beginning their search." Urilon looked towards the mouth of the cave and then at Zyi. Slipping his hand into a secreted pocket in his cloak, Urilon pulled out a small green book which was made from fresh mossy leaves with entwining dried black flowers on the cover. It was only about three inches by two and felt soft to the touch. Zyi took the book that Urilon handed to him and flicked through the pages, which were blank. Looking at Zyi, Urilon said, "This book contains the first and second creations and war in the celestial realm. It was written from the knowledge of us Jesini who know things about the past that few other mortals know. Few have ever known the history of creation and it is for you, Zyi, so you can have more understanding of the celestial war. When you have read it you will remember every word for the rest of your life, but you must only read it alone, and when you are in the dark."

Zyi thought this strange, for there seemed to be no writing, and he could not see in the dark, but he knew that Urilon knew things that he didn't, so he placed it in his trouser pocket to read at a later time.

Urilon continued to speak, addressing Niara and Zyi; "I have seen the future and there are many paths that lead to danger. I know of a certain weapon that will aid you in your quest to destroy the demon lord and the mirror of souls."

"So, we have to eliminate Nimordi?" Niara said.

"Yes, he has the knowledge to recreate the mirror of souls, if it is destroyed. So he must die, otherwise the suffering will never end." Urilon's face was calm and he then spoke a little more softly; "There is a sword, which will bring about the downfall of Nimordi. It is on a far away planet, in a temple of light that is situated in the clouds. To get inside the temple you will need the help of Nyperion, who is an elemental of the wind and is the guardian. The only way to summon him is by the use of a musical instrument called a hatana. These instruments are found all across this galaxy. It originally originated on the planet Minotane, but can be found on Solarona. The hatana is made from a precious metal only found on Minotane, and the notes are sounded by directing it at the wind and covering one of the five holes to form a sound. To summon Nyperion you will need to play a specific combination of notes and he will come to you. I do not know the sequence of sounds, but one of my kind has informed me that in a solar system in this galaxy on a planet known as Kimi, on a rocky plain, a great ice hydra dwells and she has many treasures. Among her horde of valuables is the song of Nyperion, written on a parchment." Urilon looked at Aylisha as she flitted a bit closer to him.

"The planet is not charted on any map and is only known to us Jesinis and a handful of others. We call it the planet of hidden secrets, because of the old magician who communicates with the dead and is under the spell of the ancient hydra who delves into his mind to reveal secrets of precious treasures hidden across the galaxy on other worlds. The hydra commands the magician to retrieve the items for her own private collection." Urilon paused for a moment and then continued, "You must not harm the hydra, for she is doing a service for the good, for the old man is a corrupt magic user and her spell is a form of imprisonment."

Niara and Aylisha wondered who this magician was, and Urilon then said, "To Aylisha I will give the location of the planet where the temple of light can be found." He then pressed two of his fingers together and a light shot out towards Aylisha. Being startled by the brightness Aylisha blinked about thirty times and with each blink the first impression of light she saw recreated stars that formed constellations in her field of vision, then planets appeared in various colours, until a great silvery globe in a solar system of fourteen planets lit up, and Urilon said, "It will stay in your memory and you will find the planet and the temple of light by the star map I have just given you, in the Celesta galaxy."

Niara knew now that things had become more complicated than she could have anticipated. The fate of many more lives had become paramount to justify saving one life... Zyi's. She knew that with every moment that passed people of all different races were suffering and dying because of the demon lord and the mirror of souls.

Zyi sensed Niara's aura and felt that she was perplexed about the responsibility that was now upon their shoulders, so he said, as he placed a reassuring hand on her, "There are others at risk and it is our duty to put an end to the death and suffering if it is within our power. Every moment is precious."

"Yes. Every moment we delay people die, we must follow the trail and hope we can make a difference. So we must leave now and make our way to where the rescue team are and go to Solarona to get a hatana if our quest is to be successful."

"I'm ready," said Aylisha, eager to go down the path of adventure.

"Before you go," Urilon said, "I have something for your telekin friend." Going to the back of the cave, Urilon returned with what looked like a metal ball. "It is made from a very light metal and is infused with magic." Urilon held out his hand and Muox landed on it. The metal ball unfolded itself and then wrapped around the telekin. "This will protect you," he said to Muox. The metal armour had a small visor which opened and shut at the telekin's command. Muox teleported around the cave in glee with his new material possession, the armour staying with him as he blinked in and out of space.

The company left the cave and as Aylisha flew ahead, down the rocky slope, followed by Giz, Meeky and Muox, Niara turned to Urilon, with Zyi close behind her. "One thing," she said. "You mentioned that there would be seven of us on this quest, but I only count six."

"There are seven," Urilon replied.

Niara turned to Zyi, who had stopped to face her. He smiled. 'Strange,' Niara thought and then waved to Urilon in a gesture of farewell and Urilon raised his voice, saying, "May the angels be with you."

Zyi and Niara walked down the rough, hazardous slope with no sign of the angry ghost. When they had reached the base of the mountain they all entered the rain forest and began to make their way toward where *The Mule* had originally set down for repairs, with a compass that Urilon had given them.

CHAPTER 13

It was becoming dark and the rain forest turned a shade of night, losing the vibrancy of its colourful foliage and flora.

"How are you feeling? Niara asked Zyi.
"I'm okay. The demons have stopped their tormenting, and I feel fine," Zyi answered, in a deep breath.
"Well, it seems like a miracle that the torture has ceased, you seem to be back to normal." Niara wondered just how long this would last, but didn't voice her concern, instead she said, "When they return I have the medicine that I made at the cave, just so you know that you have a choice."
"Thanks," Zyi said, appreciating Niara's forethought.
Niara had taken heed of Urilon's words and decided that if Zyi needed her help she would be able to aid him, though she still worried about this unusual reprieve from the pain and torment of the virus.

Zyi gathered some firewood while twilight was making the ground swim in shadow. Aylisha was by his side and she made a ball of fire to illuminate the area so Zyi could better see what he was looking for. After a while he had collected a bundle of debris that was not quite dry, but would have to do as the cold was beginning to surround them. Before long Niara had a blazing fire burning and giving out warmth. Giz and Meeky lay by the fire with their feet in the glowing flames and they chattered in the language of demons, as Giz had been able to learn enough of her feminine idiom to have a conversation.

Niara unwrapped a package that Urilon had given her for the trek. It contained a selection of dry food, which she picked at and offered to Zyi and Aylisha. Muox landed by her and she held out a piece of mushroom which he took between his teeth, snapped his visor shut and disappeared into the shadows to eat, out of sight of them, until he had finished; then he came back for more.
When the night was deeper and the fire was still burning Zyi conversed with Resiah, who appeared to him as an angel of light in his mind. She spoke of things that he could not remember, when he lived in the celestial realm, and about the ongoing war between the

good and evil angels. Resiah explained to Zyi that she was his guardian angel and that she lived beyond the celestial realm. Zyi eventually fell asleep and Resiah shone like a star in his mind.

When Niara awoke in the morning the fire was still burning, it was three times the size and Giz was sitting with Meeky within it. Aylisha was already flying about and had gathered some rain forest fruit for breakfast.

Walking up to Giz, Niara said, "It's lucky you haven't set the whole forest on fire."

"Well, it seems like a miracle," Giz said quite sarcastically.

Niara realized she had said the same words that Giz had reiterated to Zyi the previous evening and couldn't help admiring Giz's precocious language ability, and smiled.

Aylisha sat on a branch of a tree and ate some of the fruit she had, as Zyi awoke and sat up squinting in the bright morning light. He felt a bit sharp, as if something inside was warning him. Instinctively, he released the butterfly to hover above. In a few moments the crunching of plant material broke through the atmosphere and seven Natarkian warriors, with weapons, stepped through some dense leaved saplings and pointed their weapons at Niara and Zyi, a bit unsure as to what to make of the demons in the fire. Walking towards Zyi, one of the Natarkians stopped a few feet away and looked him over. A few words were exchanged between the warriors and they lowered their weapons and approached the fire where Giz and Meeky were. The largest of the Natarkians nodded in approval and with one gloved hand reached into the fire, his hand gripping around Meeky's neck to pull her out of the flaming fire, but Giz objected to this and blasted a smoking hole through the warrior, who was sent flying by the impact and hit the leafy floor devoid of life. Zyi knew that there was no avoiding the conflict and let loose three energy blasts from the butterfly's weapon at the unaware remaining Natarkians, stunning two with direct hits. Niara made a magic barrier between them, which made the warriors shots ineffective. The four that remained decided to make a run for it, considering that their superior was a corpse and their opponents had magic. Giz flew over the barrier and gave chase for a distance, casting walls of fire which sent them running even faster apart from two who writhed on the ground trying to smother the flames. Giz returned to sit in the fire next to Meeky. Aylisha flew down to inspect the dead male, putting a hand to her mouth so as not to breathe in the fumes of the charred body. "He's definitely dead," remarked Aylisha.

Niara turned to frown at Giz, wondering if they could have avoided the death. Obviously Giz was protective of Meeky and there was no parting them.

"I think we should get going in case more of them come," Niara said.

Zyi agreed and they left the two incapacitated Natarkians and the fire which was burning a little lower in a dug out ditch behind, heading deeper into the rain forest.

Time passed and they kept on a steady course to the coordinates. Zyi conversed with the angel Resiah about things and Niara seemed to notice that he wasn't talking very much to her, so she asked if everything was all right. He exchanged a few words to let her know he was okay. Niara wondered about the virus and wondered why it didn't seem to be active. Even though Zyi gave the impression of being quite withdrawn, at least he wasn't experiencing hallucinations.

As time continued to slowly drift further into the day, the sounds of the forest was an orchestra of bird song which gave an ambient calmness to the environment. When it was drawing towards early evening, they stopped by a great fallen tree that was covered in moss. Vines were entwined and tangled along its length.

The sunlight flickered through the dense canopy, casting shadows of soft darkness that echoed the colours of the rainbow in Zyi's vision. He knelt down to examine the dry top soil and picked up a handful to examine the insects that were there. A small creature with a spiral shell that ended in three points crawled along his hand, and he could see a blue aura emanating from it. Zyi watched as it eventually, carefully clung to the back of his hand, upside down. As he turned his hand over the creature flipped out two wings and hummed into the air with a whirring sound, and a trail of light followed it. Wondering about what had happened to him over the last several days and how a significant change had occurred from experiences that had affected his life, he thought about the extraordinary gift he had at seeing into the nature of things. Resiah spoke; "It is the life force of all things." Zyi turned to Niara, who had been watching him. She smiled and knew that he was more aware of the essence of life. Zyi went over to her and she offered him a coiled strip of a weird mushroom and said, "It is full of essential acids. Urilon knew our needs." He took the food and began to chew on it. Then Niara said, "Are you sure you're okay? You seem a little distant."

"I'm fine. I just feel different from my old self. Things have changed and I'm glad. The demons have stopped but I know they will be back."

Niara looked up as a brightly coloured bird flew overhead, then looked at Zyi, saying, "Well, it is a good sign that you are not seeing them."

Zyi's eyes flitted to Giz and Meeky who were gabbling away in another language. Niara saw where his eyes fell and said, "They're on our side. At least I hope so. Urilon is to be trusted. He knows things."

"Yeah. It's just funny. Those little demons don't scare me. It's the chanting and knowing that extreme pain is going to come." Zyi grimaced in remembrance. He then turned away from her and walked over to Muox, with a handful of nuts, offering some to the furry armoured telelin who opened its visor and allowed Zyi to drop some nuts into its mouth.

After about half an hour the sounds of twigs cracking underfoot could be heard approaching and shapes could be seen between the thick ferns and trees.

"I hope it's not more trouble," Niara commented.

Zyi landed his butterfly on an overhanging branch above, and Aylisha drew her sword, waiting behind the cover of a tree for the unknown figures to come onto the scene. Within a few minutes four humans came into view and one hailed Niara, saying, "Hello there." As they entered the small clearing the man continued to speak, "Are you from *The Mule*?"

"Yes, we are," Niara said, a smile lightening her features.

"We've been looking for you. Some of the others were not so lucky. How did you survive?" the man in charge of the team asked.

The three men and the one woman were glad to see that Niara and Zyi were all right.

"I will tell you all about it on the way back." Niara said, feeling relieved to be in the company of others that were friendly.

"We will be back within the hour," said the woman with the hand-held mini computer as she tapped a few buttons before continuing to speak, "The light craft will be here soon. They now know our location."

Giz came flying down from above, where the two little demons were cloud watching. He had Meeky on his back, and he hovered in front of the rescue crew.

"Oh, my god! Demons!" one of the men said.

"It's okay. They're with us," Zyi said.

"You can't be serious?" the female crew member said with astonishment.

"Yes. They are quite friendly once you get to know them," Aylisha said, sheathing her sword.

The rescue team observed the lesser demons for several minutes until a low humming turned their gaze skywards and a small craft came down and landed amidst the shrubbery.

A man by the name of Jon piloted the vessel and they all boarded, including Muox who was amongst the first to quickly teleport into the craft in short intervals.

"Where did that come from?" asked Jon, as the telekin zipped off with his bar of chocolate in its mouth.

"Let me guess, another one of your friends?" said the man who had been surprised to see Giz and Meeky.

"His name is Muox," Zyi replied, and then said, "He doesn't speak our language, and he is usually hungry, so don't be surprised if bits of food mysteriously disappear during our journey."

"Ok. Note taken."

The ride back was quick and soon they were all on board a much faster craft which was destined for Solarona.

As the ship sped towards its destination the crew inside were busying themselves with paperwork and communication with their superiors, to let them know they were on the way to Solarona and that Zyi and Niara were on board with two others who had been picked up.

Niara had a shower and afterwards joined Zyi in eating some hot food.

"I've gone off of meat," Zyi said, with a piece of it on his fork, left propped against the side of his plate.

"It has not come from a dead animal," Niara said, knowing that the food dispenser used natural ingredients to manufacture the meat.

"I know. But it doesn't feel right." Zyi, walked over to the food machine and looked at the menu. "Do you suggest anything?" he asked Niara.

"Try the 'noodle knot,' with soya beans and chickpeas," Aylisha suggested. "It sounds quite tasty," she added, as she looked at the list of dishes over Zyi's shoulder.

"OK," he replied.

A warm plate soon appeared with a ball of tangled noodles wrapped around the beans and peas, and some salad. Zyi ate the food and finished, satisfied that he had eaten a healthy meal.

Niara and Zyi had rooms to accommodate them. Giz and Meeky were non-sleepers and spent the night watching the nature channel on a big illusion screen. Muox slept on the table next to a bowl of popcorn. Aylisha fell asleep in Niara's room on a pillow on the chair. Zyi kept the light on at a low setting and looked up at the ceiling, lying stretched on the soft bed. His mind was active and he heard the angel Resiah speak to him. After about an hour of rest he remembered the book that Urilon had given him, so he reached into his pocket and pulled out the soft leaf booklet and turned off the light. When he opened it a pale pulsating light shone forth which formed words in mid-air and he began to read.

CHAPTER 14

The 1st Creation

In the beginning of the first creation there was nothing. Then, many eons passed and there was a great silence. And from the silence came noises and stirrings until it changed into music which formed light. The music gave the emptiness life and the life was in the form of sound. Then, the music turned into form and the first man was formed in the shape of water. Then, the water surrounded the light and the light entered the water and the man was known as God. The music was within the water and this was God's soul and he knew that it was good.

Then, the light turned the water into vapour and this was the spirit of God. The spirit of God formed his countenance and spread out and made a space. Within this space the light divided and the music left everything and formed that which was good and evil. Then God called the flames within him and they made him happy, but after a while he turned sad and out of his compassion for evil he created the love of goodness, so the evil would have a destiny. When the flames formed the ghost of death God knew that he had created a great love, for death was love's companion. The flames also created the ghost of love and the two ghosts warred. Then, God set them apart and put the music into the flames and the ghosts became silent. When the ghosts fell silent God sent them to sleep and a mist arose from them and mingled into sparks and from these sparks the generations of the first spirits were made to serve God and all the evil and good that was within them was distributed throughout his (God's) creations, his children.

The sparks of life lived in God's spirit and for the love of goodness God gave evil good and good evil, so his children would have love for one another and would grow and follow their own pathways. Eons passed and God saw that the sparks were dimming because there was more bad then good. Then, he formed the sparks into flames and this time they formed three ghosts, the ghost of death, the ghost of love and the ghost of reason. Then he called the ghost of love within himself where the music was and then he called the ghost of reason within himself and the music ceased. The ghost of death had become large and God knew that he could not call the ghost of death within him because a music that was dissonant was within the ghost of death, so he sent this ghost to sleep and the music stopped within the ghost of death and the dissonance ceased. God then turned the ghost of death into shadow and the flames that made this ghost turned black. This he called the original darkness and it was made of pure evil. Then God created the void to trap and keep the evil there until the love of goodness stirred within the shadow and good came of it. Around the void God created the abyss, this he placed within the silence of nothing, God's original place of origin. Then, God took the ghost of reason and made him guard the shadow within the abyss and the void, so the ghost of reason surrounded the abyss and nothing could enter. God took the ghost of love and divided the sparks from the flames and the original high angels were formed and God made Heaven for the high angels and knew that these would always remain truly holy and would dwell in Heaven.

The 2nd Creation

In the beginning of the second creation there was the original darkness. After a long time the darkness divided upon itself and for the first time it saw itself and knew that it was evil. Then a tremor passed through the original darkness and it began to war with the new darkness. When the two darknesses collided great fires erupted from the original one and were scattered within the new darkness. The original darkness was then called male and the new darkness, female. But the darknesses could not be destroyed. After many eons the darknesses warred and the female grew in size with all the fire within and the male darkness shrank. When the female darkness was so big it surrounded the male darkness and imprisoned him. Then, the female was called the Goddess and the male darkness inside of her was called the soul. The Goddess was good and her soul was evil, but her soul did not belong to her, it was pure evil. Many eons passed and the soul of the Goddess shaped her and she formed a covering, then the fire within her left her and formed a sea of fire around her and she shrank into the soul and the evil within her left her and went into the sea of fire. Then, the fire turned into many colours as it separated the evil within and many rays of light went into the Goddess and made a spirit within her which made her happy. Then the colours of the sea of fire turned to darknesses and they began to war upon themselves, in this way many souls were born, some were female and others were male. The first male was born from the sea of fire which was evil, but he did not know he was evil because he had no soul. But the other males born from the death of darkness were not all evil and some had fire within them and soon they had a soul within them, but their souls were female and they were evil and they shaped the males, and eventually gave them their spirit from the rays of light which had surrounded them from a sea of fire. All the males and females born of evil have no soul or spirit, but instead have a tremor within them which shapes them. And the darknesses continued to divide and the void that contained the space for the darknesses drew the good and evil from one side to the other and then folded in upon itself, creating a barrier between good and evil.

Then, all was destroyed in the final collapse, but all the spirits with souls flew into the abyss that surrounded the void and the tremors of evil remained within the collapsed void and grew in power to be turned again into a darkness. As the evil grew within the collapsed void it was influenced by the spirits in the abyss and instead of the darkness dividing again it grew a covering which was like a skin, influenced by the tremors, and this divided into many beings. The spirits flew into the abyss and left trails of vapour behind them which was the beginning of the creation of the celestial realm. The evil created the dimensions within the colapsed void which was soon made whole again, making it drift deeper into the abyss.

Thus, after much time the celestial realm and the dimensions were made. And when the abyss was full of vapour it separated from the void and the spirits were released into the vapour and became angels with a spiritual countenance and with a soul that became holy fire. The evil in the dimensions were formed into unholy fire when the void expanded into the vapour of the abyss and mingled with the celestial realm. The void expelled the evil into the abyss and the evil and good were mixed with evil souls and good ones. The countenance of the good were smiling and the evil was sad. But the good took pity on the evil and soon loved the good that the evil sometimes turned towards because of the love of goodness that was within and the evil and good created offspring. Then, the original God from the first creation came to the abyss and saw that his work was done concerning the second creation and his original creation of the first darkness.

The Celestial Realm

Now, it came to pass that the good and evil within the angels in the celestial realm remained in harmony, until one time passed when the ghost of reason surrounded the abyss where the celestial realm was, influencing the angels and bringing out their desires and natures. The angels in the celestial realm were charged with the work of creating spiritual matter to send into the void to fill it and heal the space that was within.

So, the angels in the celestial realm created worlds that would bring life into the void, and the stars would shine and bring music to the void. But, some angels had desires that were evil and they wanted to be lords and rule over the creatures that were being born in the worlds within the void. And, it came to pass that humanity, mankind was formed upon a world and some of the angels marvelled at their greatness and other angels envied their free will. Within time the angels that were inclined to evil wanted to be born into the world of humans so they could do as they please with their life and would not have to serve God. But God would not allow the inherent evil within some of the angels to be put upon the worlds. So, the evilest of angels made a plan against God, thinking that their magic powers could overthrow him and that they would rule over the celestial realm and would also populate the new worlds. But there were angels in the celestial realm that were true to God and had grown holy because God had created the love of goodness within them and they had become holy and the flame within them was good. The angels that had the evil desire to rule over the celestial realm and the newly formed worlds grouped together and were planning to war upon the God of their creation, they not knowing good properly. Thus, there began a war in the celestial realm until there was a third creation and the evil would divide and the love of goodness reign, but this was not going to happen for many millions of years as the humans would populate the universe within the void. So, the war began and the angels that were evil were cursed by God so the holy angels could recognise their adversaries and destroy the angels of evil. The evil angels had turned darker and their wings became sharper and not so rounded and they had red fire in their eyes instead of blue. So, the good angels and the evil angels fought to the death with blades of good and evil magic. The angels that were on the side of God when they were slain were reincarnated in the void to be human and the evil angels were sent into the dimensions that were formed within the void which contained ether fire which sustained their existence and shaped them into demons. The evil angels in their dimensions were separated, the males in one part and the females in another, never to really know each other unless they left their dimension and pursued the love of goodness. The evil angels that went into the dimensions formed into demons and demonettes and could only leave the dimension through a dimension slip that would release them into the mortal universe when the ghost of reason influenced their fate. If the exiled demons remained in the mortal realm they might learn goodness and eventually be taken back into the celestial realm once they regained their holiness, but if they somehow returned to the dimension they would grow into a demon lord or demonette mistress to rule over the other lesser demons. Thousands of evil angels are born into the dimensions every day and new humans are being born of the good angels.

War in the Celestial Realm

And when God cursed the evil angels, their desire for evil became stronger and they created a fissure within the abyss that ran deep within. There they took their evil and curse to dwell. Within the fissure they created many things grotesque and evil, they brought new life into the realm, creatures that were made from their magic. And the war continued and the evil grew in numbers and there was constant warring. And God blessed the good angels with clairvoyance so they would know when they were in danger. And the good angels created creatures that were good in the sight of God and they populated the abyss and were used for steads for war, and they could fly with the wounded. And the abyss was in turmoil with the war of dragons and eagles, serpents and unicorns. So, the evil angels created creatures for war that had no place in the celestial realm and were meant for the void. The creatures were shaped and mutated to serve evil and were trained to kill. And, for every evil creature that was created, the good angels created a creature to combat it. And the abyss was also filled with spiritual matter for the good creatures to eat, for they were mortal, but the evil creatures could not eat this for it was poison to them, instead they fed upon each other, which made their deformities grow and made them even more evil.

Now, God was unhappy with the abyss because it had become populated with mortality and was against his plans. But the good angels loved their creatures and took good care of them, and their creatures were loyal to them. And evil had become the breath of the fissure of the abyss and the good angels could not enter, so God created the cherubim, who were small but strong and were born from the souls of the void. And God let the souls that were good from the dead of the void incarnate into the celestial realm to serve him.

In the fissure the evil multiplied and they caused great discord. And the cherubim were sent into the fissure to destroy the evil, because they were from the void they could enter. And the evil that was once distributed within all the angels was now divided, but there was still good in evil and evil in good, but it was diluted and the good angels, although tainted with evil, could create offspring that were good and their evil would soon be no more. And although the evil angels had the love of goodness within them, this became opaque and all their offspring were evil and the love of goodness became buried within them. And the slain of the war went into the void, into the dimensions and the worlds. God cursed the evil creatures so that when they died they would become the vegetation on the worlds within the void, but the good creatures would be again with breath to be good animals of the void that would eat the vegetation within. So, the taint of worlds was to be as the evil spread within and infected life, woe be unto the creations of the angels, in the mortal realm. And the angels warred, the good angels that became truly holy in the celestial realm when they died passed through the ghost of reason and went to live in heaven. But, the evil angels that had destroyed the love of goodness within themselves went into the shadow of God and to sleep. And some of the evilest creatures that were slain reincarnated in the void as mortal creatures that fed, one upon the other. But, the cherubim that entered into the fissure within the abyss saw that the multitude of evil was great and themselves, few. So God breathed life into the ghost of reason and thus were born the fairies with magic and their alignment was neutral, so God gave them the love of justice and they were inspired to serve God, and they went into the fissure within the abyss to war with the evil angels and the fairies had powerful magic. And the fairies that were slain returned to the ghost of reason and he set them free to be a population and go into the void to be a good force amongst the taint of evil, on the worlds of men and other sentient beings.

And God taught the good angels pathways that would lead them to their fate that God had for them. And God said, "Do not stray by way of foot or wing lest you surely die. And, your pathway will be a symbol that is holy and it is also numbers that prolong your days and life. Do not follow in the footsteps or flight of others and you will surely not die." And the angels hearkened unto God and listened to his wisdom and followed their own pathways. And within their pathways the good angels learned the art of slaying, which they would use to defeat the evil angels and their creatures that they had made. And in the celestial realm the sky, the land and the light were contained within the vapour that held it together and the evil angels tried to undo the fabric so that they could destroy the realm, but God knew that it would be futile for them because the ghost of reason that surrounded the abyss poured forth its dreams that came through the holes created and many lesser ghosts came into the abyss and were drawn into the fissure that the evil angels had created and the lesser ghosts dwelt with the evil angels and they could not destroy the lesser ghosts and the lesser ghosts began to haunt the evil angels, making them angry, and the lesser ghosts went into some of the evil angels' hearts and they, the evil angels became mortal and their days were numbered and when they died they turned into a black flame and stayed within the fissure. But, there were more evil angels than lesser ghosts and God knew that the black flames would cause them to die, for any angel that touches the black flame will die and go to the dimensions. So, the evil angels made weapons from the black flames so they could number the days of the good angels. But the cherubim were unaffected by these weapons and were not afraid of the evil angels and continued to battle with them. And the evil angels created the imps to make blades and arrow tips of the black flames to use against the angels of the good. And the war continued for many thousands of years. And the lesser ghosts continued to enter the abyss and go into the fissure that the evil angels had created. And God said unto the good angels that if they did not produce offspring in the celestial realm and if they achieved true holiness by the destruction of many evil angels and of good deeds and if they followed their own path they would go to heaven if they died and there would be a soul bride for them and they would wed together and be one for all eternity.

This he promised the good angels, for they had come to loathe the evil that they fought and which was within some of them and was diminishing because of their good deeds. And it came to pass that the evil minded angels thought that they would find the footsteps of God and his pathway and undo his imprint within the vapour. And it came to pass that the evil angels undid the vapour where God's feet had passed and pure evil entered into the abyss in the form of many pure black flames. Then a high angel from heaven came through and stopped the flow of the black flames and guarded his (God's) pathway where the footprints were. And the evil angels were amazed that something else that was more holy than their once purity could exist apart from God, and the high angels could not be destroyed or harmed with their black flame weapons or any of their magic or creatures. And it came to pass that the evil angels wanted the black flames to come through with abundance, so they followed God's pathway where his feet had passed and millions of black flames came into the abyss where the high angels were not guarding and there came more high angels into the celestial realm to guard the pathway.

The good angels saw the high angels and looked upon them with admiration because they were so beautiful, and this made them look towards heaven and seek to please God so one day they would have a soul bride or soul mate. Though some of the angels that had already produced offspring became envious and turned to evil ways and slaughtered some of the good angels and their form changed and they were thus drawn into the fissure as their hearts sought to destroy the goodness in the celestial realm, and God's curse was upon them. And the war in the celestial realm is still being fought.

CHAPTER 15

Zyi closed the book after he had read the last word and the booklet exploded into a shower of rainbow sparks which lit the room momentarily. Reaching for the light panel he turned the illumination globe on, fearing that the sparks would set the room on fire, but there was no trace of any fire or ash, the only thing that was different was a floral scent he could not place, which gave him the sensation that there was another presence in the room. Then Resiah spoke; "It is true. The war is still being fought."

Zyi let the knowledge slowly sink in and thought about what it was like in the celestial realm where there is a war going on. Eventually, tiredness overcame him and he fell asleep without noticing that he had fallen asleep.

In the morning Niara and Aylisha were the first to wake. They went to the main lounge for breakfast where Giz and Meeky were watching the horror channel. Muox was bouncing up and down on a cushion that was made of some sort of elastic. Niara approached the two little demons and said, "It's a bit early for gore. Can you put something a little less disturbing on?"
"Only thing worth watching," said Giz.
"What do you mean? There must be something else on." Niara picked up the remote and put on the cartoon channel, "Now that's more like it for you two."
"Boring," said Giz, who now had a wider vocabulary from watching so much.
"At your age you must find it enjoyable," Niara said, as Meeky let off a giggle when a giant rabbit hopped onto a mushroom and began swaying this way and that way until it fell off.
"I'm over three million years old," replied Giz, trying to look unamused.
"And I'm the wicked goat of the north," Niara said, implying that she did not believe him.
"Anyway," said Giz. "I know how make apple crumble."
"Oh. That sounds nice. Well you can give it a try after lunch," Niara said, amazed that the lesser demon could be so good with his speech.
Aylisha sat near the screen to watch the cartoon, and occasionally

let out a laugh at the absurdity of the humour.

Zyi awoke about an hour later and came into the lounge area where most of the ship's crew were talking about things. He sat down and Niara came over with a bowl of wheat triangles in chocolate milk.

"Thanks," he said, and began to eat with an illusion wand which could assume different shapes.

"How was your sleep?" asked Niara.

"Okay. I saw many things in my dreams that are difficult to put into words."

"Dreams are often like that. At Dimo, my homeworld, there are dream interpreters who translate the language of dreams for us to understand. There are many symbols in dreams that relate to the real world and they are seen as a way of furthering the development of us mortals, on our spiritual pathway." Niara smiled warmly.

Aylisha landed on the suspended table, picked up a piece of popcorn from the bowl and began chewing on it.

"So, how did you two meet?" asked Zyi, looking from Niara to Aylisha.

Aylisha continued to take little bites from the popcorn she held, which was massively out of proportion to her tiny hands, compared to humans. Then she said, "I searched for Niara for well over three years, after a visionary from one of my kind, the soothsayer, saw in the future that Niara would find the orb of Alluvian. The orb was once made a long time ago to trap one of our kind who had turned toward the darkness, he had become evil. Some thought that it was a spell cast upon him by demons, others believed that it was innate. This orb that was created was stolen from our citadel and the prisoner was released. My father Urial has been unlawfully imprisoned inside the orb and it has been taken away and hidden far from our world. It has been over a thousand years since I have seen my father." Aylisha looked at Zyi and he could see and sense the sadness in her.

Niara spoke. "We'll find him," she promised.

"I know," replied the fairy.

They sat in silence for a little while until Muox returned from scouting the ship and landed in the popcorn, face down. There followed a series of munching sounds and the bowl was soon empty and the telekin's belly full.

Hours passed; Niara and Zyi sat talking as Giz prepared the dessert they were all looking forward to. After a fair amount of time had gone by Giz presented them with a browned dish that smelt wholesome and after they had eaten it, they agreed that it was an exceptional apple crumble.

The time on the quick flying craft went by smoothly and soon one of the crew informed them that they were approaching solar system 328, where the planet Solarona was the fifth planet from the sun.
The pilot was soon setting the craft down on a platform in a spaceport.
"This is Amenis, part of the western continent. You will be taken to a guest house where your belongings will be given back to you from *The Mule*. The owners of *The mule* have paid for you to stay there for two weeks, at their expense, as a token of apology for the unexpected delay of your arrival."
"Thanks," Zyi said.

Niara smiled and Aylisha flew into her pouch. Muox followed just behind, teleporting through the space at short intervals. Giz and Meeky were between Zyi and Niara as they walked off the ship and into a transport cube. The air was subtly warm for the time of evening and soon they were in a smart hotel thirty floors high. Niara and Aylisha had one room, while Giz, Meeky, Muox and Zyi had a larger room next door. Their belongings were brought to them the next morning.
When the sun was in the sky they decided to explore the city and try to locate a hatana. Zyi was a bit irate because Giz and Meeky had kept him up most of the night as they watched the entertainment console.

The air was clean and Niara, Zyi and Aylisha went for a walk in the great city. Long streets with market stalls selling wares of all sorts adorned the walkways which were in the shadows of the tall buildings away from the glaring heat of the sun. There were many people walking the streets and a lot of them were species from other planets. Niara stopped by a table and picked up a bracelet made from sparkling tree sap, fashioned into heart shapes. Finding the artefact to her liking she paid the woman three shinara and continued to walk, slipping it on her wrist.
A cool breeze washed over them as they continued along the procession of people making their way around the market. As they were approaching the main plaza where the restaurants were a soft

sound could be heard, it was a mixture of notes which combined to make a pleasant sensation to the ear in a hauntingly ethereal, ambient way. The sounds came from a stall where a young boy was with his grandmother and several instruments were displayed on the table's surface. In the boy's hand was a long metal tube, about eight inches long, and he held it to the breeze, allowing the wind to pass through. His dexterous fingers played over the apertures of the hatana and the notes were sounded, making a melody that carried through the surrounding area.

Aylisha said, "That must be what we are looking for."

"I think so," replied Niara.

They stopped and enquired. Indeed, it was the instrument called a hatana and Niara paid sixty shinara for it. The young boy wrapped the instrument in a silky orange fabric and secured it with a deep red cord.

The trio sat down at a table in the square and soon someone arrived with a tray laden with food and two glasses of water. Tasting the food, Zyi found it to his liking, and Niara assured him it was meat free.

A demonling, the size of a thumbnail, flew under the table with a little pouch around his waist. He peered over the table making sure he wasn't seen. An emissary for Nimordi, he quickly shot towards Zyi's glass and dropped a microscopic centipede into the water, then darted away. No-one noticed the incident and Zyi picked up the glass of water to drink.

"No! Don't drink the water," Resiah the angel said in Zyi's mind.

"What," thought Zyi. "There's nothing wrong with it." Holding the glass up he looked at the transparent liquid and could not see the minuscule centipede.

"What's wrong?" asked Niara.

"Oh, it's nothing," he replied and took a long drink.

"You shouldn't have drunk the water, now things will change. I will not be around for a while, for the demon lord has tricked you." Resiah spoke with a hint of sadness in her voice.

"It should be all right. It's only water," Zyi thought.

"You will have to learn to trust me. I know things that have consequences," Resiah replied.

Zyi looked at the water again and thought that it looked normal. Resiah's concern seemed unnecessary.

After they had finished their food and drinks they walked for another hour and Aylisha bought a new green dress at a clothes store for other races. Zyi stopped where a stand held cards. He looked through them and thought that they were quite morbid, showing pictures of coffins and gruesome deaths. "What do these cards say?" he asked Niara, who was familiar with the language.

"Oh, they're happy death cards. It is a local custom for people to send their relatives a card wishing them a happy death."

"But this one looks like torture," he exclaimed in horror.

"I think how the custom goes is that the more gruesome the message the better chances of longevity."

"How strange," he thought to himself, and then continued on.

Returning to the guest house they found the lesser demons and Muox still in Zyi's room watching the visuals. Sitting down in his room Niara informed Zyi that her space craft was further up north and would take them a few hours to reach via local transport. "Be ready in half an hour and we will set off," Niara said and then returned to her room with Aylisha.

The next half an hour went really slowly for Zyi, and after the first twenty minutes the chanting started and Nimordi's voice could be heard. "It is time to suffer." A series of pin-like stabbing pains in his legs shocked him into realizing something was wrong. Then about six lesser demons jumped out of the walls and started to slice him. So he ran out of the room, blasting small charges as he went from the butterfly's weapons, damaging the walls. He was soon out of the building and in the city, being chased by demons.

Niara heard the commotion and realized that Zyi had begun to experience the hallucinations again and that the weapon was active. "Come on Aylisha, we must find him."

Aylisha and Niara separated in search of Zyi. Each had a tablet for him so he could regain his normal composure and be free from torment. It was about an hour before Niara found him being led by some of the local law enforcement officers to a transport vehicle. Niara rushed up to them and said she was a friend.

"Sorry, but he has to come with us for assessment. He might have a mental illness, or a form of disease," the man said.

Niara cast a spell to confuse the men that were trying to escort Zyi, and they released their grip on him. Niara took him back to the hotel and he swallowed the tablet on the way. By the time they had reached his room he was back to normal and Aylisha returned shortly afterwards.

"We must leave right away, before the law find out what's going on," Niara said to Zyi and Aylisha. Within minutes they were all out the door with their possessions and in a transport sphere, heading for the northern spaceport.

Upon reaching their destination Niara handed over her identification to allow them into the area where her space craft awaited. They approached a slim silver vessel sixteen metres by thirty. Niara pressed a button on her key pad and the side entrance opened, slotting out and down a smooth ramp for them to ascend. Within moments they lifted off as silently as a feather in the breeze and slipped noiselessly into the sky.

Inside, there were four rooms. The smallest was for the pilot who sat upon a soft morph seat which allowed for flexibility. His name was Xeroni 6 and he was a state of the art machine with a vast amount of knowledge stored within his enhanced memory banks.

Giz and Meeky made themselves comfortable in one of the back rooms. There was a holo-screen and it was instantly activated as soon as Giz tapped the screen console.

Aylisha was sleepy and flew up to a suspended hammock which was hung from the ceiling, where Niara had positioned it during their journey to Earth.

In the control room Xeroni 6 responded to Niara's questions when she asked about the planet Kimi, and where it was located. "It will take us twelve hours at a medium flight rate to reach from out current position. It is in the Ranius solar system and the planet is inhabited by a few settlements of humans and kios. Due to the harsh atmosphere there are formidable winds and heat waves, which makes it uninviting."

"Take us there," Niara asked, and Xeroni 6 skimmed a few lights on the illuminated grid and said, "Done."

"I need some rest," Zyi said. "It was a shock to experience the awake nightmare again. I thought it was under control."

"It was unfortunate. Though you were lucky to not have suffered more, it defies explanation," Niara said, knowing that at least the medicine worked at double the dosage.

Zyi sat back on a padded seat where a pile of magazines lay. He picked one up and perused it, looking at the colour pages which depicted scenes of Earth and different cultures found on the planet. The writing was unfamiliar, but looked interesting, being made up of symbols. Niara sat down next to him and said, "I was familiarizing myself with your home world. Better to be prepared for the unexpected. It is not in my language. I picked up the magazines on a planet called Reazinea, just to see the pictures. Xeroni 6 translated the words."

Zyi tossed the magazine down. "It looks better than it actually is."

"Isn't that always the same though?" Niara said.

"I suppose. It's just that there was a picture of the green hills of my childhood against a blue sky, and the thing is, that part of the world is usually subject to a lot of rain. There is also an industrial mining facility there, so you sometimes hear explosions that disturb the tranquility of the place. The only reason that it is a tourist attraction is because all throughout the year, except January, there is a festival which brings in a lot of people."

"Looks can be deceptive, especially if you wanted to get away from it all," Niara said, half smiling.

"Anyway, where did you learn to speak English so well?" Zyi asked suddenly, realising that it wasn't Niara's mother tongue.

"With the aid of magic. We have an extensive catalogue of languages on my home world, and I learnt how to speak it by memorizing the dictionary and the intonations, using a mnemonic spell. It will last about seven years before it degrades, but by then, if I keep using it, seventy percent will be retained."

"Interesting," said Zyi.

CHAPTER 16

The journey to Kimi was fairly quick, considering that Niara's craft had supreme technology and it was going at a leisurely speed.

A whorl of sand rose in gusts as their vessel came to rest on the edge of a desert. Ahead lay a vast rocky plain with a pinnacle of ice pointing towards the sky, its magnificent height visible from where the group were, nearly six miles from the icy abode of the great ice hydra.

"I think our presence should go unnoticed until we reach the hydra's crystal palace," said Niara.

"I hope you're right," Aylisha said. "I've heard fables of these creatures and they are formidable, and quite rightly feared by our race. They have magical powers that increase with age, and they are rumoured to live to well over a hundred thousand years."

Thoughts were going through Niara's mind about how they could get the red parchment with the song of Nyperion upon it. Zyi walked mostly in silence calling out in his mind, Resiah, Resiah... But there was no sound of her voice.

As they drew nearer they reached the edge of a great basin some three miles wide, and the glistening fortress of the ice hydra looked awesome.

"It looks like a gigantic meteorite created it," Zyi said as they all began their descent down the rough slope.

"Could well be," Niara said, feeling sure that it was.

"There's no sign of the hydra yet," Aylisha said in a voice lower in volume than normal, as they drew closer to the structure.

"My bet is that she'll be inside," Giz remarked, and continued to speak, saying, "I'm sure not as scary as you make me out to be."

Aylisha shot Giz a frown and said, "Believe me, these creatures are fearsome and if you want to stay alive, beware."

Meeky grasped Giz's hand tighter and said, "Oh, no."

Approaching the giant abode, a grand archway towered above them and was sculpted with intricate knot work. Zyi and Niara paused for breath at the sheer grandeur of the designs. Then, without a word said they entered. Zyi released the butterfly in stealth mode into the space in front and above.

A great circular chamber, miles in expanse, welcomed them with a chilly bite in the air, making their breath misty. "I've never seen anything like it," exclaimed Zyi, as he wondered how it was constructed. Rows of statues lined the circumference of the great room.

"They're not made of ice," Niara said. "They were living at one point. These are some of treasures of the great hydra."

Zyi, drew a deep breath as the realization hit him. "There must be over a thousand different species here, immortalized in ice."

"Welcome to my palace," came a raspy voice from above, as the great hydra flew down to land before them. Aylisha drew her rune sword and years of hatred yearned for her to attack the creature.

"A fairy," hissed the hydra. "You will make a fine addition to my collection."

"You will die first," seethed Aylisha, knowing full well of the history between their two races, and pointing her sword at the great creature.

"I think my magic will overpower your puny blade." The hydra glared with bared teeth.

"We are not here to harm you," came Niara's calm voice, and she looked at Aylisha with an admonishing glance. The fairy sheathed her brandished sword and huffed in agreement with Niara's words.

"So, what are you here for?" questioned the hydra. "And what makes you so sure that you will leave alive?"

Zyi felt the threat in the creature's tone and it sent a wave of dread through him. With a few quick motions of his fingers, unseen by the hydra, the butterfly landed on one of its scales and unfolded a cannon from its armoury, ready for any eventuality.

"We need your help," Niara said, hoping that her straightforwardness and honesty were the best way.

A drop of liquid metallic copper fell from somewhere above, landing by Zyi's foot. He glanced down and then looked up to see a brief glimpse of something moving upon one of the great ledges.

"And what is it that you want?" the hydra asked in a manner that held a hint of mockery.

"We understand that you have something in your treasure horde that is of great use to us and by letting us have it you would be saving many lives."

"What may this be that you're seeking that I have? And what makes you think that I will give it away freely?"

"There is a piece of parchment with some writing upon it that we need. The parchment is made from dry red leaves and is extremely important to us."

"I know what it is that you seek, but it has been stolen from me by someone by the name of Alluvian."

Aylisha gasped in astonishment. "Alluvian, you've seen him?"

"Yes. He is powerful for one his size. It took me by surprise, and he will surely die if he is caught. At this very moment, my pet magician Zeni is searching for him. He has ways of finding things that are not meant to be found."

"It looks like we've wasted our time coming here," Zyi put in.

The hydra bellowed with laughter, "I don't think so, human. Now you are all here, you will stay." The great hydra let out a blast of ice too fast for Aylisha to avoid and the fairy was encased in a block of ice, falling to the floor with a crystalline clink. Niara brought forth a wall of flames between them, then made it rise to the height of the palace. It started to lick the surface of the ceiling, but to no effect.

The great ice hydra blasted bolts of ice at the barrier, passing through the curtain of fire unscathed and narrowly missing its targets. There was a gust of wind behind them and Zyi turned to see a male hydra lash out at him to grip around his body with a great clawed grasp. Zyi was lifted up from the floor and could hear his ribs crack under the pressure. Niara looked up in disbelief. Urilon had not mentioned another hydra. The male ice hydra blinked an eye at Zyi as he held him close, "You will make a fine trophy."

Zyi struggled for air and managed to say, "I will die first."

"That you surely will," the hydra affirmed.

Then, a young ice hydra flew down from above and hovered by his father. Coppery marks were stained on its icy scales and there was slow dripping from an unseen wound. The young hydra spoke to his elder and the male released the pressure on Zyi, and spoke; "It is fortunate for you that my young one wishes you alive."

Giz, looked at the young hydra and said, "Can we sit your back?" Giz still held Meeky's hand. The young ice hydra could not understand the language and flew down to rest on the ground near his father.

Niara withdrew her hands from the air. She was anticipating the next move, ready to cast another spell. Zyi was released onto the crystal floor; he rolled and lay there unconscious. Niara ran to him and picked up the cold form of Aylisha on the way. Cradling his head she looked up and said angrily, "Why did you attack us? We are no threat to you."

"It is in our nature not to trust," the male ice hydra replied.

The wall of flames lowered and the feminine creature came over and spoke in her tongue to her son. Then, she said, "I misjudged your intentions. And I didn't know."

"Didn't know what?" came Niara's bitter voice, full of contempt.

"That you were sent here to aid us."

"Why do you need our help?" Her voice softened.

"My son was wounded by Alluvian's blade and it had poison. He is slowly dying."

The young hydra flapped one wing and more of his metallic blood splashed onto the floor.

Giz was a bit disappointed when the young ice hydra ignored his request and decided to go for a flight with Meeky on his back, totally unaware of any threat that the great creatures could pose.

"I will only help you if you free Aylisha the fairy and give us your word that you will aid us." Niara looked at the female hydra, looking for any sign of treachery in her eyes. The female creature then said, "We will help you if you can rid our son of his illness."

Niara held Aylisha in her hand and the hydra breathed an orange mist on her; the ice evaporated, releasing the fairy from her icy prison. Aylisha stirred; her eyes flicked open and her wings flitted in a series of impulses, then she rose into the air and scowled at the great ice hydra that had frozen her.

"They have promised to aid us if we help heal their young one," Niara said to the fairy.

"I don't trust her," was Aylisha's response.

"We don't have much choice." Then Niara knelt down to attend to Zyi who was coming around.

"What happened?" was his first concern.

"It's all right," Niara reassured him. "We are out of danger's way."

"My ribs.. I think one is broken."

Niara placed her hand above his chest and with a few words a tingling force vibrated into Zyi; in a matter of moments he felt the bones knitting back together.

Niara then turned to look at the young ice hydra who was resting, neck stretched along the smooth surface of the ground. She rose, approached him and said that she would try to neutralize the poison. After several minutes she sighed and said, "It is a strong venom. I have not encountered this type before and I am afraid I can't do much to aid him. Aylisha, you try."

Unwillingly, Aylisha the fairy flew over and inspected the youthful hydra. "His wounds are indicative of a rare snake's poison found on my home world. It causes the skin to open and not heal. I know that if it is the venom I think it is then Alluvian came here with the purpose of death." She then proceeded to cast a few spells which began to heal the wounds. Then Aylisha reached into her pouch and pulled out a purple petal from a flower she had picked on Zarkon. "If this contains the chemical I think it does, then it should help destroy the effects of the poison. I need some water."

Zyi handed over a water flask and the fairy poured a little into the cap and dropped the petal into it. Upon close inspection, Zyi noticed the petal sink and release a golden solution into the surrounding liquid.

"Tongue out," Aylisha requested of the young hydra. He complied and his translucent tongue flipped out and she poured the contents of the cap onto it; he whipped it back in with a grimace.

"That should do it , " she said.

Niara then spoke up, "We have kept our side of the bargain. Now what can you do for us?"

"Zeni should be here within a few weeks; he will have the parchment and Alluvian. You will be given what you ask if your friend's healing is successful," the female hydra let out a breath of compromise she was not used to.

"And if he does not improve, you will surely be statues," the great male hydra put in.

Zyi spoke to Niara in a low voice; "People are dying as we speak. Is there no other way?"

"We need the parchment. All we can do is wait. We have no alternative."

A sound of rumbling could be heard from outside and the great feminine ice hydra said, "Ah! the *plasmodium* is here, sooner than I anticipated. Zeni has returned."

After several minutes of eager expectation a wizened man with long black hair walked in through the impressive entrance followed by two dusty, dry skeletons, one carrying a sack over one shoulder blade. "We have visitors?" the man said in a condescending tone. Then, raising his left hand to show a red parchment, "I have returned with Nyperion's song, and the diamond of Korinth, which I didn't realize the sneaky fairy had stolen while my back was turned. That bloody Alluvian sliced my hand off," he cursed and raised his right arm where there was no hand.

"And you let him get away?" came the harsh voice of the elder male hydra.

"I had no option. He just disappeared."

"You're lucky I don't turn you to ice on the spot," the great male growled.

"Oh, I'm far too valuable to turn to another boring statue," Zeni said in a nonchalant manner.

The female hydra concealed amusement and the elder male blasted a head off one of the skeletons with an ice bolt. The skeleton then proceeded to retrieve his skull.

Giz and Meeky appeared from above, Meeky on Giz's back. "There's a lot of treasure up there," Giz stated.

"Oh, a lesser demon," exclaimed Zeni. "I believe there is a need for a statue like you."

"I'm not in the mood to set fire you today. But if you threaten me again you will have a hole in your head bigger than your mouth," Giz smirked.

"He talks as well! What a rare find," he remarked, totally ignoring the little demon's wit.

"There is no threat. I will abide by my promise," came the feminine ice hydra's voice. "Give the parchment to the woman," she ordered Zeni.

"After all my trouble," he complained.

Niara took the red scroll and placed it in her belt pouch. Zyi looked satisfied, and said, "Well, we will be leaving now all is settled."

"Not so fast," said the imposing male ice hydra. "We want to be sure that our son is well for at least three weeks, before you depart." The young hydra looked up with a sparkle in his eye, knowing to some degree what was said. "I am healed. My blood has stopped flowing from the wounds and my body has lost the pain. They are free to leave. We owe them my life. I was soon to die but now I'm saved."

The youthful hydra's mother felt a wave of happiness and brushed a claw over her son's head and said to Aylisha, "You have done us a kindness, please forgive me, you are free to leave."

"Let's go," Niara said to Zyi, Aylisha, Muox and the two lesser demons, with a certain relief. They walked out of the palace and the hydras watched them go. Zeni ordered the skeletons to prepare some sustenance for him. Niara and Zyi passed Zeni's craft, with *The Plasmodium* in black lettering on the wings.

"I think he stole the craft from the space mutant thieves," Niara said.

"What makes you say that?" Zyi enquired.

"It's because the thieves have a mother ship called *The Mosquito*, which is hidden somewhere in my galaxy. They are wanted for many crimes and are known to send their plasmodium crafts out to ambush cargo vessels. They are considered to be parasites."

CHAPTER 17

The slim sliver craft lifted off the planet Kimi and ascended into the sky.

Giz and Meeky sat next to each other upon a soft morph couch. Their skin had become wrinkly and they needed a blast of real fire to feel better.

"We need fire," Giz requested of Zyi.

"I don't know what we can do about it," Zyi said, and then went to the other room to ask Niara if there was any way to give the little demons what they needed.

"There may be some materials in the storage compartment that we can use to make fire with. I will have a look," Niara said. Within ten minutes she had returned with two lamps and a fire torch. "I think we can use these."

The two lesser demons who looked rather older than they usually did were taken to the back of the craft, and Zyi poured the flammable liquid from the lamps all over them and proceeded to set them alight with the fire torch. They both went up in flames in a sudden blaze and Meeky jumped up and down in excitement. After several minutes the flames went out and their skin was smooth again.

"Thanks," said Giz, grateful for the pleasure. "It makes us feel lot better."

Meeky smiled and said something in her own tongue to say thank you.

In the main rest room Zyi was reading a biology magazine in his own language when Niara sat next to him. Aylisha flew down and rested by them.

"We must go to the Celesta galaxy and locate the planet that is in the star map in my memory," Aylisha said.

Niara thought a little before saying, "Well, once we reach my home system of stars we will be that much closer to finding this mysterious planet."

"Yes," continued Aylisha. "And even though we will be close to Dimo it would be wise to follow Urilon's advice and try and get the sword first."

"I agree," Niara said without hesitation and turned to Zyi who nodded in acquiescence with the Jesini's instructions in mind.

Xeroni 6's voice came out of the grid speaker which was set into the wall. "Niara! There are twelve *plasmodium* crafts coming up on the screen and they are bearing down fast."

"Looks like we've got company. And not the sort I like," Niara said, rising up from the couch.

"The mutant thieves," exclaimed Aylisha.

Giz, picking up on the danger, said, "Can we blow them up?"

Striding out of the room to go to see the threat on the screen Niara answered Giz's question; "We don't have the weapons."

"No weapons!" Zyi stated in disbelief. "We're sitting targets."

Reaching the control room Niara looked up at the display of the thieves' space crafts as they lined up alongside the S*lipstream,* and a voice came over the communications console with the twisted face of the mutant commander. "We're taking your cargo and if you try to resist we will blow you to smithereens."

"Straight to the point," Giz said, admiring the man's audacity.

"We have nothing of value," Niara replied.

"Then we'll take your craft. Prepare to be boarded."

The screen returned to the short and long range scanners as the communication was terminated. Xeroni 6 tapped a few illusions and the craft began to vibrate slightly. "Evasive manoeuvres?" he asked of Niara.

"Yes. Toward Celesta."

The mutant leader commanded his men to approach the S*lipstream* and board her, with instructions to take the prisoners alive. Then he looked up at the visual field to view his prize, but it was not there. "Where have they gone?" he bellowed.

"Sorry, but they seem to have disappeared," came a squawky, feathery mutant's voice.

"You better be joking or you're gonna be roasted over a fire," the commander warned.

"But sir... There's nothing we can do. They're gone," the avid mutant said in a pleading manner.

"Aria! Mal!" the man in charge said, pointing to two of his fellow bandits, one a man the other a plump woman with tendrils. "Take him away. He's tonight's supper, and use the Krusian stuffing." The mutant commander slumped back on his seat and contemplated the main course that he had been planning for a while. Staring out into the open space on the viewer, he half said to himself, "Bloody technology."

The swift, slim craft that was constructed on Dimo glided through a time river which allowed the ship to skip along a line, like a pebble skimmed on water, and miss spaces between them and their destination, making the journey to Celesta in a fraction of the time it would have taken.

The spiral arms of the galaxy before him took Zyi's breath away as he looked on in wonder. Meeky stared out at the beautiful sight of all the stars in their glorious setting.

"It looks small," Giz said, a comment that came from ignorance, for he had never seen space like this before.

"Believe me Giz, it has millions of stars and we have seen countless different forms of life that are on many of the planets." Niara assured him that there was more to it than a picture on a ship's visual system.

"Now, we have a slight problem. The star map Urilon gave me can only be interpreted correctly if we are in the right place, because depending on where you are in the galaxy the stars are different," Aylisha said, feeling lost.

"Well, the database on board can give us the constellations of the stars in surround vision. Though it could take a long time for you to locate the precise positioning," Niara said, rubbing her shoulder. Aylisha flew onto a cushioned chair saying, "Hit the lights!" They all left the fairy in the dark with the computer flicking through the star maps of Celesta, with pinpricks of light all around her glimmering.

A few hours passed and Zyi spoke to Niara, voicing his concern. "How long do you think it will take her to locate the right configuration?"

"It could take days, weeks or even months."

"The thing is people are suffering and dying as we speak. We must find a way to speed up the process." Zyi placed his warm herb tea on a surface.

"There is no other way, unless we can go to Dimo where the resources are more efficient. But Urilon did advise against this until we have the sword."

"Then we must trust him."

Aylisha zipped into the room quite breathless; "I've found it!"

"Already!. It has only been two hours," came Niara's reply. Muox was bouncing up and down, obviously infected by the fairy's excitement.

"Yes. Come and see." Aylisha led them into the control room where the stars were fixed. "There!" the fairy pointed to a star. "That's the one where the planet is. It's the sixth one from the sun."

"Are you sure?" Zyi asked.

"Of course. The stars align perfectly with the mental image I have of the map."

"Well," said Niara, tapping the pale golden illusions of the control grid, "We are on the way now."

The speedy craft turned slightly and then sped toward the fixed location.

The time it took to reach the solar system where the mysterious green planet was seemed to only take a few moments, though several hours had passed.

The misty, emerald atmosphere came into view as they went through it and a serene sensation of peace could be felt as the ship made its way to the planet's surface. "Make the ship transparent," she instructed Xeroni 6. "It's so beautiful," said Niara, gazing at the scenery when the craft flew over the thick wooded areas gliding through the twilight sunset, with a constant speed for about an hour, until reaching a range of mountains with snow adorning them. "Fly to a moderate climate with mountains and grasslands and make it early afternoon," Niara commanded Xeroni 6 when she had enjoyed the beauty of the extended sunset experience through the transparent ship's body.

"Seven minutes and we will be touching down," Xeroni replied as he tapped some illuminated controls.

The warm sun felt soft on their skin as they left the space faring ship and stepped onto foreign ground. Above them great white clouds lazily drifted by, making billowy shapes which transformed themselves with the breeze.

"Well ,we're here," Giz said, hovering with Meeky on his back.

"Now where shall we call Nyperion?" Aylisha asked.

"Well, Urilon said somewhere up high," answered Niara.

"Looks like we'll be climbing that mountain," Giz said, pointing towards the great range of snowy peaks.

"Yes," Zyi agreed.

After a lengthy walk when many hours had passed they were up quite high and Niara said, "I think that this is as far as I can walk, bearing in mind the journey back."

"It's cold enough," Aylisha said, with small wisps of breath escaping from her mouth.

Zyi, pulled out the hatana from his pack and unrolled the parchment with Nyperion's song in black ink. Holding the musical instrument and looking at the finger positions on the scroll he held it out to the gentle breeze which made a low earthy sound as his fingers changed to cover different holes. A beautiful melody made by the seven notes which sounded angelic carried in the air and Niara noticed a whorl of mist spin around and descend from up high. Nyperion, his form an ethereal shape brighter than white with patches of gold, which formed the details of his features, was floating before them and when he spoke his voice had the same timbre of the notes of the hatana but more dreamy. "Why have you summoned me?"
"We need something from the temple of light," Zyi said, in awe of the magnificence of the elemental.
"No one has been there for over a thousand years, and there is a price to pay if you want to enter."
"Name your price," Zyi stated, doubtful that he would be able to obtain what this great spirit would ask of them.
Nyperion looked at the telekin who had the visor down to keep warm and said, "I wish for the creature to sing the song of the winds in its language."

Niara turned to Zyi, who smiled and reached out to Muox and tapped his armour. The telekin flipped the visor up and blinked at Zyi. "I want you to follow the sounds of this instument," Zyi requested of him. Muox hummed a few notes in reply and Zyi began to play the hatana, repeating the sequence. Muox murmured the tune and then became clearer with the music. Nyperion lightened up as if the sun was shining within him. "Thank you," he whispered, then it started to snow. Within minutes a shape had formed from the falling flakes of snow, sticking to an unseen impression, and a white silhouette of a winged horse with a chariot had come to life. The elemental wind mounted the horse. Turning to the group he said, "Only one will pass through the gateway of the temple."

Zyi stepped onto the chariot hearing a crispy crunching sound as his boots felt the firmness of the snow vehicle. They then sped into the sky. It was below zero and they must have been flying for about thirty minutes but Zyi did not feel the chill of the wind. A shining golden light could be seen up ahead as they approached a stretch of cloud. Passing through an archway of light the snow pegasus came to a halt where a flight of stairs led up, winding out of sight. "Follow the steps, but remember only take one thing from the room or you will surely die."

Walking up the glistening stairway he soon came to an opening where two shining statues, one male the other female, stood with spears crossed. As he drew closer the two figures withdrew their weapons to let him pass. Inside the great room with cloudy walls, secured by lines of sunlight, there were many great treasures. Destructive weapons of power, some magical others futuristic, hung in mid air. He looked at some delicately inlaid sword hilts and wondered which one could be the one he was looking for. Reaching out to touch one he heard his angel say, "No. Do not touch. That is not the one."

Zyi withdrew his hand, glad that his angel was now back with him, and walked along, looking at the great swords that were lined up. The angel Resiah said no to each one that he thought could be what he was searching for. When he had looked at all the weapons in the room Resiah said, "Leave now."

"But, we haven't the sword," Zyi felt cheated, but followed the advice, knowing that his angel knew things he didn't. Passing a great war hammer with glowing inscriptions, he noticed a table. Upon this table was a crystal vase with a fresh yellow rose. "Take the flower," Resiah said. So Zyi picked up the rose and left the room. Upon seeing what Zyi had, Nyperion smiled and said, "You have chosen wisely."

They mounted the pegasus and chariot and flew off into the sky. Nyperion gave Zyi a word of advice; "Throw one petal at a time into running water and all will be revealed."

Zyi thought this mysterious, but things hadn't been that straightforward since he had met Niara.

The winged horse of snow landed back on the mountain and Niara saw the rose and remarked, "You haven't the sword?"

"It will soon be with us. We must trust the angels."

The snow chariot and horse then collapsed onto the ground in a puff of flakes, then Nyperion spoke, with a hint of Muox's song in his voice, saying, "May the good spirits guide you." Then he swirled into a whirlwind of snow and dispersed into the air above.

CHAPTER 18

It was night by the time they reached Niara's space craft. They had been walking in the light of two small bright flames conjured by magic from Niara and Aylisha. Once inside the vessel they ate and sipped at a hot beverage. "We can fly to a flowing river or stream where it will be daytime," Niara suggested.

"Okay," came Zyi's reply, and he pondered the significance of the yellow rose that was on the table in front of them.

After they had regained some energy the ship landed by a winding river making its way through a lush meadow dotted with wild fruit trees that attracted small creatures. Zyi approached holding the thorny stalk of the rose between his index finger and thumb. Standing by the meandering waters Zyi plucked a gold petal from the flower and slowly outstretched his arm; after a slight pause he dropped it into the river. The petal hit the surface and stayed, fixed. Zyi continued to drop the rest of the flower's petals into the rushing water. One by one they turned crimson and a light shone from them forming strands which came together, spinning and weaving until the sword named *demonslayer* glowed a blood red brightness and was suspended in front of him. Clasping his hand around the hilt of the sword he held it, pointing towards the sun. It felt light in his hand and he could sense something like a heartbeat coming from within it as if it were alive. Giz looked at the weapon and said, "That is a powerful weapon... Even in dreams." Zyi did not fully understand what the lesser demon had meant, but was glad that they were that much closer along the path of their quest that would end the suffering of the innocent.

Back inside the S*lipstream* the coordinates were set for the next location, Dimo.

"There still remains the question of how we are to find the demon lord Nimordi. There are thousands of dimensions; how are we to travel there?" Aylisha voiced her concern as to whether there was any real hope in chasing after nightmares if they couldn't be seen.

"Well," Niara said, "I know that there have been voyages to these dimensions. We have a machine that will allow us to enter into the realm of demons, even though their material nature is different. We have designed special fabrics that can withstand the ether and heat. Though we must find out which of the demons' abodes will have the mirror of souls so we can destroy it and Nimordi who has the knowledge to construct them."

Zyi turned his face toward Aylisha then to Niara and said, "Didn't Urilon say something about the little demon with wings, Giz, being of some use to us? Maybe he has a memory of his dimension which we can use to locate it."

"I had thought of that," Niara said, and continued, "If he wouldn't object we could transfer his history and try to find a way to achieve what we need to know and do."

Meeky was making an over sized plasticine demonling and Giz sat watching the visual display unit when the craft touched down on Niara's home world Dimo. As they exited the vessel Zyi could see a vast city of unfamiliar buildings that rose high with walkways and floating gardens. Winged creatures flew about unconcerned with other metal air faring machines. It was nearing late afternoon and Niara said, "Welcome to Armaricia... The city of jewels."

"It's amazing," Zyi said in open admiration of the sheer beauty of the contrast between urbanization and rural simplicity.

They took a speeder vehicle to the complex of Niara's reisidence where there was food and shelter among the other people that lived there. "We will have a few days rest before going to the institute of research where we can try to discover more, and also to destroy the virus that is within you. You should be safe until then. Just keep taking the tablets," Niara said to Zyi, knowing that now that they had reached her world he was safe.

Zyi Mercurial sat in his room pondering over the past and talking to Resiah, his angel. Eventually he lay down and closed his eyes. When he opened them again it was dark and he could hear whispering voices of demons. Several little demons emerged in his field of vision. 'They can't hurt me,' he thought. Then one of them stuck its ether sword into him and he felt the pain. He instinctively reached for the sword and six more lesser demons appeared and began to attack him. Swinging the sword at them he severed limbs and heads. The little aggressive demons drew back in surprise as their fallen disappeared in smoke. Then, more appeared and overwhelmed him so he ran out into the night of the city. Fleeing into a garden, up some steps, he turned to see a horde of the lesser demons close on his trail. 'I will fight them in the park,' he thought. The trees in the garden had their roots in the air with jewels of light which hung where fruit would have been; they glowed. The little demons were on him and he fought with vigour and determination, sending them to their death with quick, sharp cuts of the sword. Niara appeared with a friend of hers. Using their magic they could see what he was up against and with a small hand held device shot a yellow flare into him, sealing off the connection to the mirror of souls. He collapsed in fatigue and the two women came over to him.

"I'm so sorry," said Niara to comfort him. "I thought you'd be safe, but they must have broken through."

A small crowd of sentient beings from all different races gathered around. "I saw them," one said. "There were so many."

"You must be gifted, to see the nightmares of others," Niara's friend said.

"We must go to the institute. I know it's late but there is no other option, this is urgent." Niara took Zyi's arm while he held *demonslayer* pointing down towards the ground.

At the research facility Zyi was taken to a room with four different lights facing him as he sat in a chair. In front of these were lamps with rotating filters and he felt the warm, soft light enter his body. Lightning flashed through him and the whispering evil murmurings fell silent, then he heard Resiah's voice saying, "Their work is done."

A low green light came on and Niara entered the room. Zyi's eyes became focused again and covering the walls of the room were impressions of demons with swords and malicious smiles. There must have hundreds of them. "They were the ones that were within you but now you are purged of them," Niara said seriously. He looked around in horror, thinking about how unclean he had been with all the evil that had manifested itself within him. "So it is done?" Zyi enquired.

"Yes. You can never be affected again."

Zyi said "You have been a true friend."

She smiled warmly and replied, "It is my duty to serve the less fortunate."

They left the establishment and after a night's rest awoke the following day. Niara took Zyi and the two little demons to the institute of research at Zyi's request, for they had little time. "Every day that goes by more innocent lives are being put to death and tortured. We have to put an end to it." Zyi knew what people would be going through as he spoke, being empathic since he had experienced the DNA weapon.

CHAPTER 19

The morning of the next day was bright and warm. As the creatures sang strange music just outside the open window, Niara came into the main rest room. "You must see this," she exclaimed, and with a command word a visual image appeared with images of a man being led into what looked like a court room. "That," she said, "Is Theo Grey. He is being put on trial for crimes against life. The evidence gathered by some of our specialists have shown that he is responsible for genocide on many different races of life. I caught the news earlier. He was also one of the engineers of the DNA weapon which is against the egalitarian act 545446. The justice agents from this world tracked him down through several life times and are now bringing him the punishment he deserves. Nothing can escape justice, not even death," Niara said quite passionately and slightly angrily.

Zyi looked at the face of the man and thought it looked familiar. Then, an image of the man, with a ball of fire instead of an eye, came into view and it all became clear. Niara turned the language on for Zyi to understand and the news reporter continued saying," And Theo Grey is being brought to trial at last. He was responsible for the creation of the DNA weapon known as project Stealthblade which has caused suffering throughout the known universe to many a life form. He was tracked down to a planet in the milky way called Earth and our team of detectives arrested him there. He will be paying the price for his crimes in this life and many future ones to bring justice for the many beings that has suffered this terrible weapon. There are others that were involved with this project who are now being pursued and in time they will be caught and punished." Niara switched off the screen, sat down and looked at Zyi, wondering what was going through his mind.

They ate some breakfast and Niara then took him by foot to the Institute of Research where Aylisha, Giz and Meeky were. "They are searching Giz's memories at the moment and there will be a report in a little while, but first I want to show you a film of reincarnation to help you understand that there is life beyond death." Niara put a hand on his shoulder and continued, saying, "Maybe it will convince you."

"I have some faith about it now I have experienced spiritual things, but I am still sceptical," he said quite seriously.

Niara led him to a room where there were seats and headsets. Tapping a few buttons she said, "Put this on." Zyi placed the device around his head and pictures came to life with someone speaking in his language.

The film showed the energies of a person which was interpreted as spirit. During the course of the documentary Zyi followed a person's life and death; watching the spirit flow from a dead shell into the universe, slipping though a warp field and into the ghost of reason where it was eventually drawn from to be fused into a new life and thus reborn. It amazed him that this could be real, and he believed it now because he knew auras existed and it was the spirit of life, also the book Urilon had given him he knew to be true. Placing the headset down once the film had finished, he left the room in search of Niara. She was just on her way to see him with two hot brews in her hands, "So what do you think?" she said.

"It is astounding and I believe you now 100%. It has confirmed some of my suspicions." Zyi felt elated because now it was affirmed that really life is immortal and that his parents were still alive... somewhere.

"Let's go and check up on Giz," she said as Aylisha came flying up to them quite breathless. "Come and see what we've found out," the fairy said. "You'll not believe it."

In one of the main research rooms Giz was surrounded by machines and was on fire to ease his thought processes. Meeky sat on a fireproof cushion with flame lamps on either side.

"Giz is still under observation," a student of the sciences said, "But we have a lot of information about him, though not of any dimensions as yet." Holding a portable object which projected a screen the woman started to tell them about Giz's life as she showed them the visuals that went with it.

"Giz was once an angel who lived in the celestial realm. There, he fought in the war. Once on the side of God, he fought the dark angels and was a mighty warrior. What turned Giz to become part of the forces of darkness was that his lover was brutally murdered by the demon lord Nimordi who was once an evil angel. How this happened was on one fateful day when Giz was following his pathway, the pathway given to each angel that they must follow to stay alive. Giz was slaying the dark angels when he saw his love

Ameia, who often crossed his path, leave her trail to save a child that had wandered off the path and there were two dark angels that would have taken the child's life because they were cruel, when Ameia intervened and left the safety of her pathway to rescue the child. Giz noticed more dark angels grouping and they were swooping down to attack the child and Ameia. Giz flew off his trail and went to assist her but it was too late; Nimordi slew her right in front of him with a black flame sword and let off a laugh of pleasure when she fell to her knees, dead. Giz fought and killed several of the dark angels but Nimordi escaped when Giz's strength and skill was better than his. Giz took the child and returned to his path, then returned to his dwelling place with the child. The child's parents had been slain so Giz raised the child as his own. The child was named Zyiaron. Giz knew that Ameia would be reborn in the dimensions because she was slain by a black flame weapon, her memory of the celestial realm would be forgotten because of the nature of the black flames, unlike the other demons that were slain by the angels of light, whose memory would be intact.

Giz then thought long and hard about Ameia. He learnt that the dimensions were separated into male and female dominions and that it would be many thousands of years before Ameia could return to the celestial realm. Ameia would have to cleanse herself of the taint of the black flame, which would involve her leaving her dimension and experiencing water in the mortal universe which would open her soul to her original innocence and give her back some of her memories. Giz searched for Nimordi the dark angel every time he was on his pathway fighting, and would leave his trail to avenge Ameia's death to slay Nimordi if he had to.

Many years passed as Zyiaron grew under the care of Giz, and he taught the art of slaying to Zyiaron. Zyiaron killed Nimordi in a battle where he was wounded by Nimordi's magic but was not defeated. Giz's heart grew heavy over time and he longed to be with Ameia. He knew that he might not see her for many thousands of years, possibly millions of years. So when Giz discovered that the demons retained their memory when they were slain when they were sent down to the dimensions, he ruminated upon turning to the darkness of evil. Giz was not evil, but he thought that the only way to see Ameia again was to commit evil acts and be slain by an angel of light to be sent to the dimensions. It was the only way to find

Ameia and be with her without losing his memory. Eventually he would find and kill Nimordi in the dimensions to banish him to the ghost of reason where he would sleep till the end of time to be awaited to be judged. Giz turned to forbidden magic so he would slowly turn evil and rebel against the angels of light, but he was wise about this so he would only have evil to serve his purpose until his ends were met to slay the angels of light, and then he would be slain and sent to the dimensions of ether fire. Over several hundred years his inner light turned to darkness and he began to be misshapen and dwelt in the fissure where he would venture forth to slay the angels of light until his innocence had diminished and he knew it was time to die. Giz fell under the blade of an angel of light and was sent down to the dimensions where he would live in the dominion of the demon lord Nimordi. Meeky is Ameia, he has found her after all this time though a great fire within him burns for vengeance..." The woman's voice trailed off.

"And Zyiaron is me," said Zyi. "I was the child that was saved."

"Yes. You are that one," the researcher said.

"Well, that was unexpected. I never knew those things had happened." Zyi turned to look at Giz who was still under the spell of the machines and whispered a silent prayer of thanks.

Niara then spoke up, looking at Meeky, "That explains their fondness."

Aylisha agreed and the machines slowed to a low whine. The female scientist scanned through the information that was coming through the metallic green machine. "Here we have it. Dimension Y122." The woman smiled and turned to Niara. "I will send the coordinates into the dimension voyager and you can leave in location room 26."

Giz sat up with his ether sword still in his hand. "Lets go get him then!"

CHAPTER 20

There was a bright green light and then everything became clear. They were all standing on firm ground, upon a hill, in a small ring of light which marked the spot where they could return back to Dimo. Upon a rise in the terrain on their left was a film of liquid fire. "That is the portal of death. It leads to the ghost of reason," Giz said, for he knew this dimension.

The scene below them was of blazing fire and smoke. Lakes boiled with molten liquid and the fumes were swirling around in quickening spirals. Zyi placed his hand around the respirator he was wearing to make sure it was firmly in place. The fields that surrounded them were protecting them from the heat and thick air. Niara spoke, saying, "It is worse than I could have possibly imagined. This is surely hell."
"I have had dreams of this place. Look up there." Zyi pointed to a great tower that had jagged edges and twisted spires. "It must be where the demon lord dwells."
Giz looked at the great tower and pointed to it with his ether sword, saying, "Nimordi can be found there."
Aylisha then spoke, saying, "It looks too far away to get there undetected." There could be seen writhing hordes of lesser demons and clouds of demonlings down below indulging in some sort of ritual, which blocked their pathway. Giz then said, "There is the way. Follow me." Making their way around the back of the hill down into a forest of trees that had leaves of flame, Giz took them deeper into it. "We seem to be heading away from it. Where are you taking us Giz?" asked Niara.
"Trust me," came Giz's reply.
Soon they came to a great statue of three lesser demons that were renowned for their evil. Giz then pulled at one of the hands and the statue slid aside to reveal steps leading down into the darkness. "Follow me," Giz said.
They all descended into the gloom with two strands of liquid fire flowing down the pathway which led deep underground, which lit the way. They followed the tunnel for about two hours until they reached a lake of fire that spanned about a hundred metres. "How are we going to get across it?" asked Zyi, knowing that his equipment would not work in this dimension and all he could trust

was *demonslayer,* his sword.

Niara spoke, saying, "It won't be a problem." She waved her hand and Zyi and herself were lifted off the ground and were transported across the lake to the other side as if they had wings. Aylisha flew next to them and the telekin blinked across. Meeky took Giz's hand and both were over in moments. They resumed their route through the underground tunnel system for what seemed like several more hours until Giz said, "We're there." He stopped and pointed upwards with his ether sword. High above them was an opening and yellow light could be seen burning there.

"Another flying spell would be useful here, " Zyi hinted to Niara.

"Of course," she replied and with a few magical words they began to fly up towards the light. Upon entering a great room lit by flaming balls of yellow fire Zyi and Niara landed on the ground, Aylisha next to them drawing her sword that emanated a green glow, which could be heard humming slightly. The great room was adorned with skulls, from ground to ceiling, of all different races, demons among them. "This place is eerie," remarked Niara. "I've never seen anything like it."

"This way," Giz said, marching towards a great doorway where stones of different shades of red glimmered in the light; they were adorning the edges. The rest followed and found themselves on a balcony that over looked the great expanse of a hall where on the far end a great throne was made of bones that were stained with blood. Upon it sat Nimordi the great demon lord, behind him the great mirror of souls dwarfed everything below. There were hundreds of lesser demons within, with chalices of fire water in their hands, drinking to enjoy the pleasure that the liquid fire gave them. Suspended high above a pool of lava that flowed rivers of fire around the throne was a great orb that shone white, and Zyi immediately sensed the pain coming from it. Aylisha gasped in horror; "It's the orb of Alluvian."

"I know," said Niara. "We will free your father when we have dealt with Nimordi." As the last word left Niara's lips the great demon lord looked up at them and gave a tremendous evil laugh. "At last we meet again, pitiful humans," his voice boomed across the vast expanse of the hall. "And it looks like you've brought some friends with you to your deaths." Nimordi stood and said in the demons' language to the lesser demons, "Kill them. But leave the male human to me." The horde of lesser demons below started to surge up the stairs to attack them as the demon lord watched from his throne. The first horde to emerge onto the balcony received a wall of *pain fire* from Giz's magic as the lesser demon charged at them. Niara said to Zyi, "We must go down into the hall and fight from there." She grabbed Zyi's arm and they levitated down into the mass of little demons. Zyi, sword in hand, landed and sliced three of the demons in one fell swoop. Niara blasted them with various spells that she had been trained to use at a young age, searing and killing demons in seconds.

Aylisha dealt with some of the flying lesser demons that attacked her, slicing them within seconds of one another. The telekin, with visor down, flitted around Zyi in flashes of light. Several lesser demons jumped onto Meeky and one raised his ether sword to cut her neck, when Giz blasted him with purple fire and took Meeky and flew to the orb of Alluvian where she stayed out of harms way sitting on top. Giz then rejoined the battle. As the battle unfolded the demon lord watched with amusement as many a lesser demon was slain, for the great demon took pleasure in death whether it was kin or foe. Zyi and Niara destroyed the little demons that were intent on harming them until they made most of the way across the grand hall. Then Nimordi cast a wave of intense hell fire across the expanse in front of him which swept with a roar across the hall, killing many lesser demons that were in the way. As it neared Zyi and Niara it curved and caught Niara who had her back turned in combat, knocking her to the ground as a flood of darkness overcame her. Aylisha, seeing this, swooped down by her side and cast a high level barrier spell around her so the lesser demons could not kill her, for she was still breathing. Nimordi laughed victoriously as he shot out a ray of energy that lifted Zyi from the ground and brought him to face the maniacal demon lord. "At last the time for your life to end is near. I have enjoyed making you suffer," Nimordi said, releasing the energy that binded Zyi.

"Your time is at an end Nimordi. I have come to deliver vengeance for all the souls you have murdered and tortured." Zyi gritted his teeth and held *demonslayer* up and pointed it at Nimordi.

"You are no threat to *me*. The only one with enough power to slay me will never be seen again. He is destined for an eternity of darkness." Nimordi let out a brief laugh.

"And that would be my father Urial," said Aylisha, who was now by Zyi, her rune sword shining an emerald glow. Lifting up her hands she directed a stream of light towards the orb of Alluvian, hoping to damage the force that kept her father imprisoned, so that he might escape. Nimordi looked bemused. "There is no chance that you can free him with your limited power. Only my brother could have the magical ability to release him, and he is dead. Your father has not seen the light of day for over a thousand years and it will remain that way."

Aylisha tried with all her strength, but to no avail. The orb of Alluvian remained unscathed. Zyi then charged towards Nimordi, leaping over a rivulet of lava with *demonslayer* arcing down upon the demon lord. Nimordi was quick and raised his hand and Zyi froze in mid-air. "Your petty mortal strength is no match for mine," the demon lord said and Zyi felt an immense pain enter his being and, collapsing to the ground, he let out a scream of agony. Giz came flying over and Aylisha said, "We must all attack at once." Giz let off an assault of ether blades at the demon lord and Aylisha cast a blinding spell on him. Nimordi was surprised at this offense and fell off his throne as his sight was taken away and sharp ether spikes pierced his skin. He let out a howl of rage. "Now Zyi," cried Aylisha, "Finish him."
Zyi, raised demonslayer and was about to leap on Nimordi and drive the sword into his heart when he heard the voice of Resiah saying, "No Zyi. You will not kill him that way. Throw your sword in the lava." Zyi, stopped and lowered his sword. He had learnt to trust the angel Resiah with his life and knew that she was always right, so he threw aside the sword into the lava. "What have you done?" Aylisha said in horror. "That was the only chance we had of destroying him!"
"Ha. Ha. Ha," came the laughing voice of Nimordi. "You didn't really think your pathetic magic was strong enough to blind me did you?" Nimordi waved his hand and a bolt of invisible force hit Aylisha and she instantly went blind and put her hands to her eyes in astonishment and pain. Muox flew over to her and Nimordi, upon seeing the telekin, looked puzzled and then terrified. "What is that doing in here? The prophecy must not be fulfilled." With that the great demon lord let out a blast of energy at Muox which sent him spinning into the stonework at the far end of the hall, where it was lodged in its armour.
Demonslayer began to dissolve in the lava and the fumes rose up under the orb of Alluvian. Giz raised his hand to cast another

assault of ether blades but the demon lord held him with his immense magic and said, "You have defied me for the last time Giz, now you will feel the pain of death at my command."

"You are destined to die Nimordi, for all the suffering you have caused in my life before your descent in the celestial realm." Giz harboured great enmity for his foe, whom he had once served under as a pseudo ally. Giz let forth all his hatred in a deadly spell that burnt into Nimordi's chest. The demon lord held the magic force and then lashed out at Giz, sending him into a state of shock which left him on his knees staring ahead in wonderment.

Nimordi turned to Zyi. "Now, mortal, it is time to die. I have had enough amusement from you." Nimordi raised his fist and a swirling red mist was manifested around it, which then descended down towards Zyi, but a silver light protected him. "What is this?" Nimordi said in bewilderment.

"It has been a long time, demon lord," came a voice from above. Urial was hovering where the orb of Alluvian used to be and Meeky had jumped down and was trying to break the spell Giz was under by pinching him.

"No! It cannot be!" Nimordi exclaimed in fear.

"Yes. I am free. The soul of your brother Heminion was within the sword and the essence of it released me from the prison." Urial then saw his daughter Aylisha and he said a word which travelled to her and made her see again. "Father. It has been so long. We thought you dead." Aylisha flew up beside him. "Now, I will destroy you," Urial said, raising his hands in a gesture of a great spell. Nimordi blasted a flare of deadly ether fire at Urial and the two energies from the adversaries met between them, but slowly Urial's magic fire forced back Nimordi's spell and with more power the pink fire of Urial's magic blasted into Nimordi and filled him on the inside, consuming the evil life within. Nimordi slumped back lifeless as his skin started to bubble and blister and wither until his being became ash. Niara came round and stood up, shaking dust off as Giz snapped out of the enchantment spell and all around them the other demons had started to fight each other with claw and blade. All hell was let loose as the demon lord's power diminished the control of its subjects which resulted in pandemonium.

"We must destroy the mirror of souls," Niara said as they approached the great expanse of the silvery reflection.

"We cannot. Not without the aid of a telekin," Urial said

sorrowfully.

"Muox, where's Muox?" Zyi started in earnest as he looked around. Aylisha's keen sight spotted him embedded in the wall and she flew over to see if he was still alive. Upon reaching him she could see he was not awake, so she tapped on his visor and soon enough a few musical notes emerged from the metallic armour that had protected him from the heat and force of the demon lord.

"The God of all seeing is with us," said Urial under his breath. "We are indeed fortunate."

Muox teleported to where the great throne was, into Zyi's outstretched hands. "You're safe. I thought we'd lost you."

The telekin blinked out a few notes and the two of them turned to face the mirror. Muox jumped into the space near the mirror of souls and beeped a few notes. The essence of the mirror's silver thread started to undo and the telekin flashed in and out of space along the length of the mirror, unwinding the coil that held the power of the souls' torment within, and faces appeared and dissipated on its reflection. All across the universe the peoples of its target that were countless billions were eased from their suffering as the weapon was slowly becoming ineffective, releasing the pain from the minds of the targeted individuals. Zyi felt a great weight being lifted off his shoulders as Muox had unravelled the last of the deadly mirror. There was a long thread of metallic silver which ignited at both ends and began to burn at an extreme pace until it met in the middle within the space of a prolonged moment. There was a loud crack as the power finally extinguished and a great peace descended on the universe. "Well done Muox. We couldn't have done it without you," Zyi remarked with a smile.

"Let's get out of here," Niara said with a sense of relief.

Urial transported them outside and they made their way to the ring of light where they could return home. Giz and Meeky turned to the others and the winged one said, "We will not be going back. We must go to a new life." He took off the flaming blue mask and discarded it.

"What do you mean?" questioned Niara.

"It must be done," was Giz's reply and the two lesser demons walked away towards the portal of death.

CHAPTER 21

At the dawn of war in the celestial realm the angels of light are lined up with swords of white fire flaming holiness. Unicorns breathe misty air and stamp the ground. Eagles with white feathers circle the space above, awaiting a command.

Silently watching angels of death with blackened wings peer out of the great fissure, red embers burning in their eyes. A sound of broken harmonies fills the air, starting off faint then reaching a crescendo of dissonance and a swarm of evil emerges from their hiding place, led by skeletal dragons of doom, black as midnight with thorned skulls and claws of razor sharp black flames.

The angels of light await the sign and soon, as the horde of chaos sweeps across the plain, a turquoise star is seen shooting across the sky and descends down into the battle field, the benign angels rising with pleasant harmonies to dispel the discord, shaped to put uncertainty and hesitation into the angels of light. With the star shining the war takes shape with the evil black flamed blades slicing, hacking and being countered by the benevolent beings who dance a war dance following the path they were instructed to follow in flight and footsteps. Ambidextrous flashes of white blades sent souls to the lower dimensions.

Great four headed snakes with mutated wings soared across the sky and battled with the eagles where many were killed. Magic was ablaze from the hands of fairies who fought deep into the fissure with the companionship of the cherubim who were strong, faithful and true with their swords.

A female angel of light fought with one sword of shining holy brightness which had slain many, when she saw a lone child and advancing were two angels of death, so she left her pathway to save the boy. "Don't leave your pathway," came the shout of another angel with two white flamed swords. But she could not leave the child to die. The two dark angels confronted her in battle and she slew one, then several more appeared and the male angel of light left his pathway to assist his love, but almost upon reaching her he saw one of the evilest angels slay her with a black flamed sword.

The male angel of light let out a cry and charged in, eyes burning a fierce blue, slaying all the evil apart from the one who dealt the killing blow to the female angel of light. This dark angel could not match his skill and flew off at a great speed in defeat. Seeing his loved one dissipate he picked up the child and flew to a safer part of the realm where the boy would be safe before returning to the war.

END CHAPTER X

Giz and Meeky walked hand in hand towards the liquid portal which led to death and the ghost of reason. As they approached their reflections were visible and they both formed tears that ran down their faces. They both closed their eyes briefly as they were about to enter, then Giz turned to Zyi and said, "Nimordi hated you, even as a child, because he knew that one day you would have what he wanted, the high angel that was meant for you. When your life has come to an end here you surely will achieve true holiness and will live in heaven with Resiah your soul bride. It is part of the plan." Feeling the warmth that radiated from the great portal, a smile formed on their faces and within a moment they had entered and there was a golden flash as they were consumed. Niara turned to Zyi, not really knowing exactly what Giz had meant, and said, "It's what they wanted. They were meant to be together."

Zyi smiled a half smile in sadness and said, "I know. It is sad to see how love has taken them. But, they will be judged and their goodness will be known so they will be reborn. I'm sure that our paths will cross again."

The company then stepped into the circle of light and were transported back to Dimo, where their lives would continue with the knowledge that they had put an end to a lot of suffering and that millions were saved from the haunting of Nimordi and the mirror of souls, though the war in the celestial realm was still being fought.